TWO STEADFAST ORPHAN'S DREAMS

RACHEL DOWNING

CORNERSTONETALES.COM

THE ORPHAN STAR OF THE DOCKYARD

TWO STEADFAST ORPHAN'S DREAMS: PART I

CHAPTER 1

No one could ever call it glamorous, but to young Miss Isabella Thorne, age seven and a quarter, the side streets near her house in Liverpool were a stage, and she was always ready to perform. With an old piece of rope from her father's docking yard around her neck as a necklace, and knotted pieces of string forming rings on her fingers, she held her dusty skirt like it was made of the finest silk, and threw her head back in overwrought agony.

"Oh, woe is me!" she said, in a high-pitched voice. "My true love has betrayed me!"

"Ha ha ha," said the girl standing opposite her, without much enthusiasm. "Now your riches are all mine!"

Isabella hesitated, and then snapped out of her performance, frowning. "No, Elizabeth, you're doing it again. I *told* you. You can't just say it. You need to *act* it. Put on a deep voice, like this." She rearranged her face into a villainous scowl, and when she spoke again, it was in a rich, deep voice, full of menace. "Now, my love, your riches are all mine!"

Sitting on the side of the road nearby, Isabella's younger sister, Tabitha, giggled. She was only two, so it was almost impossible to get her to perform, but she was Isabella's best audience member. She always laughed when Isabella put on her voices, and she loved the songs that Isabella would invent, making her sing them over and over until she knew all the words too. This was sometimes a challenge for Isabella, who, until recently, had only ever come up with her songs off the top of her head, and could hardly remember the words or the tune from five seconds ago, but Tabitha's devoted enthusiasm – along with her noisy tears when Isabella admitted she had forgotten the song – inspired Isabella to take a little more time over her words, and to commit them to memory before singing them whenever her little sister was about.

And Tabitha was always about these days. With their father hard at work at the docks at all hours and their mother always tired with the new baby growing in her belly, it fell more and more to Isabella to keep her sister entertained so their mother could rest. But Isabella did not mind. She loved her baby sister, and every time she thought of the new sibling that she would get to meet any day now, she felt a little shiver of excitement. Mamma would be even busier after the baby came, and Isabella would have to entertain Tabitha *and* look after her new sibling when she could, but she loved her sister more than anything -- would even fight Timmy Woodhouse from down the street if he insulted her, and *had*, despite him being almost ten and much bigger than her – and was certain that the new addition, whoever he or she may be, would be just as wonderful as they grew.

The other girl at the scene, Elizabeth Morley, was her best friend, small and spindly with blonde hair and a long nose. Her father had gotten into trade, and had made something of a name for himself in Liverpool in recent years, so Elizabeth's dresses were always a little finer than Isabella's, her shoes a little newer. But even if Isabella's family was not rich, she had never heard them worry about money, and the idea that they *could* worry had never occurred to her. Her father had a fairly important position at the docks, for a labourer at least, and if there were any monetary concerns to be had, they never reached Isabella's ears. She knew that Elizabeth's father did not necessarily encourage the friendship between the two, and that they were not to play *too* near Elizabeth's house, but at seven, that fact didn't concern her. Isabella's main concern regarding their friendship was that Elizabeth did not have a shred of theatrical instinct, and if Isabella wanted to move from one-off song and routine to putting on *stories*, she needed someone else to perform with. Elizabeth was her best friend, so it made perfect sense for them to work together. In fact, Isabella would consider it a betrayal to perform with anyone else. They had been practicing for hours now, and Elizabeth was yet to remember to put on a voice, and she had not even attempted a villainous laugh.

"I'm tired," Elizabeth said finally, collapsing to the ground with a definite pout. "Can't we go do something else now, Izzy? Why don't we go to Mrs Hancock's? It's nearly the end of the day. She might give us some bits of cake if we're lucky."

"We have to get this right, Elizabeth," Isabella said importantly, but Tabitha had overheard Elizabeth's suggestion, and she, at least, thought cake to be an excellent idea. "Cake!" she shouted happily, stumbling to her feet. "Cake!"

"See?" Elizabeth said. "Tabby wants some too. Come *on*, Izzy. Don't we *deserve* something sweet after all this work? I bet Mrs Hancock will give us something if you sing a good song for her. She always does."

Isabella really would have preferred to keep practicing, but she could not deny her best friend or her baby sister, not when they both looked so pleading. "All right," she said, with as much dignity as she could muster. "We shall go. But we have to practice again tomorrow, Elizabeth, and you have to promise to try to do the voice."

"I will, I promise!" Elizabeth said, with all the conviction of a girl who was no longer listening now that she had gotten her way. She grabbed Isabella's hand and tugged. "Come on!"

As it turned out, Mrs Hancock had just received an order for a rather large and expensive cake from a very refined-seeming woman, and was in an excellent mood. As payment for Isabella's song, she gave them all the ample cake crumbs that had fallen from the day's creations, and the girls sat on the ground outside her shop, crumbs collected in their skirts, and giggled and ate until every last mote of sugar had been licked from their fingers.

The sun was setting by the time Isabella and Tabitha turned for home. Their mother would probably scold Isabella if they were late for dinner, but Isabella did not think it was quite that late yet, and she always had entertaining Tabitha as her defence. As long as she kept her younger sister safe and happy, their mother could usually be persuaded.

As they reached the street on which they lived, Isabella felt a prickle of apprehension down the back of her spine. She could not have said why, exactly, but something in the air felt *wrong*, like the world had shifted without her noticing it. The street was strangely quiet, except for the unbroken shriek of a baby. Isabella tightened her grip on Tabitha's hand and found herself slowing down her footsteps as she approached their home. It took her a moment to realise that the baby's cries were coming from inside.

Her new sibling! Isabella's heart leapt at the thought, and her first instinct was to run barrelling inside the house, but something held her back. The baby cried and cried, and she could hear no one else, no sign of her Mamma's voice, no fussing of a neighbour. Something was terribly wrong, and Isabella felt certain that as soon as she stepped inside the house, that truth would change things forever. She squeezed her younger sister's hand. She had heard whispers, when the grown-ups did not think she was listening, of women who died while giving birth to their babies. If the baby was crying alone, did that mean that Mamma...?

Isabella pushed open the door and stepped inside. The room inside was dark, the curtains drawn and the lamps unlit. Isabella led Tabitha through the house, following the sound of the baby's cries. They were coming from the bedroom. The door stood slightly ajar. Heart hammering, Isabella nudged it open.

The baby lay on the left side of her parents' bed, wrapped in blankets, its face red from howling. Mamma lay beside it, staring up at the ceiling, and Isabella felt a rush of relief. Her chest was rising and falling, her eyes open. There was no blood on her that she could see. Her Mamma was alive.

But Mamma lay completely still, ignoring the baby's cries. Her hair was tangled around her head, and her face was ghostly pale.

"Mamma?" Isabella said. She dropped Tabitha's hand. Tabitha must have felt the darkness in the house too, because she did not rush to their Mamma's side, but continued to stand beside Isabella, staring. "What's wrong, Mamma?"

Their mamma turned her head to look at them. "Isabella," she said, her voice hollow.

"Mamma." Isabella ran to her mamma's side of the bed and grabbed her arm. "What's happened?"

"Your father," Mamma said dully. "He's dead."

CHAPTER 2

No one wished to tell Isabella exactly what had happened to her father, but she overhead enough, when neighbours came around to check on her mother. There had been an accident at the docks. Her father had become caught between two boats, and although no one ever said exactly what had happened, Isabella had a vivid imagination, and she came to her own conclusions. She lay awake at night, imagining one ship at her back, another moving irrepressibly forward, its weight pressing into her.

Tabitha did not understand where their father had gone. She kept asking for him, and no matter how often Isabella told her that their Papa was not coming back, she continued to demand they show her where he was.

After her initial shock, Mamma kept herself busy caring for the new baby, a little sister for Isabella and Tabitha that she named Abigail. Neighbours came to the house to help at first, but they had their own concerns, and gradually their support faded. They were lucky, Mamma told Isabella, after Tabitha had gone to sleep one night. Papa had been a hardworking, sensible man, and he had saved a little money for the family, should disaster ever strike. They were not destitute, but the money was not near enough to sustain them for long. They could not afford the rent on their house, so they would be forced to move somewhere cheaper, and Mamma would need to take on as much work as possible, doing laundry and mending for richer ladies, while caring for Abigail. She gained a little extra work, partly due to the sympathy people felt towards a new young widow, but even this was not enough to provide for them.

The new house was a single room, crammed in the slums with hundreds of other one-room hovels. Isabella did her best to help her mother keep it clean and tidy, but the stench of refuse from the street pervaded the air, and damp seeped through the walls. Even then, her mother's income was not enough to pay rent and also buy food, and with winter approaching, they would freeze without money for a little fuel for the fire. The sort of women willing to pay Mamma to wash and mend for them were not willing to have their clothes worked on in such a place as they now lived. They complained that the stench of poverty got into the material, damaging them worse than they were before they were sent for mending, and Mamma found it harder and harder to find work. The work she could do outside the house was limited by the need to care for Abigail, and although Isabella would have abandoned everything to care for her baby sister if she could, only their Mamma could feed her.

Which was how Isabella, now age eight, ended up finding employment in a butcher's shop with an old friend of her father's. He could not afford to pay her much –

and who would pay a significant amount, for a small child's work? – and the hours were long and hard, but she brought home enough money to keep her family fed and off the streets, and that was enough. Mr. Hardstone, the butcher, was a somewhat dour, serious man who did not speak much, but Isabella appreciated his presence. He did not ask her to do any of the butchering herself, only required her to keep the place clean, so Isabella spent many long hours scrubbing blood from the tables and the floors, her hands cracking and bleeding, themselves. At first, she tried to distract herself with inventing little songs as she worked, but Mr Hardstone demanded quiet, and she found that her heart was not in the invention anyway. There was very little to sing about in this new world without her father, working so hard she was barely able to see her sisters or her Mamma, spending every scrap of energy she had to try and keep them all alive. Even if she had had any time to play, she had lost her best friend when they moved to the slums, Elizabeth's father forbidding the friendship, as though his family would be tainted by association. Sometimes, Isabella was overcome by anger at the injustice of the situation, at her father for dying, at the world for letting him, at her mamma for moving them, at little Abigail for needing so much. But later Isabella would calm down again, and she would feel ashamed for her thoughts. She was lucky that she could help support her family, and she would not choose otherwise, not for anything. She saw now, all around her, what happened to those without the ability to work, those who could not support themselves. They were the lucky ones, and she could not forget that.

 The years passed, and Isabella continued to work to support her family. When she was twelve, she managed to earn a job working in a cafe, hired by one of Mr Hardstone's customers, and although she had to hide her place of residence and her new boss was far more prone to shouting than the butcher, her cleaning work was blood-free, and she received the same pay for taking orders and carrying trays, rather than scrubbing the floors until her hands and knees were raw.

 When Isabella was fifteen, her mother's cough, which had plagued her for years, began to bring up blood. Mamma insisted that she was fine, but eventually, Isabella insisted that she see a doctor, for Tabitha and Abigail's sakes, if not for her own. The doctor, although kind, could do little to help. Consumption, he said, probably caused by the bad air of the slums. The best cure they could hope for would be to move somewhere with fresher air, but with Mamma unable to work, they could barely afford their current home, let alone anywhere healthier.

From that moment on, her mother was often weak and delirious, and Isabella struggled to work to maintain them all while also caring for Mamma and her younger sisters. She did not want to have to send Tabitha or Abigail off to work at the butcher's like she had had to do at such a young age, and the cafe owner refused to hire anyone so young and inexperienced.

So Isabella worked as her mother faded. The years passed quickly, with Isabella too busy to really notice the passing of the weeks and months, and Mamma clung onto life, weak but breathing. Tabitha found work too, so that they could buy the occasional medicine to help Mamma, but nothing seemed to help her for long. She would get a little more colour into her cheeks for a few days, and talk to them about memories of when they were small, when their father was alive, but she would weaken again quickly, leaving the sisters frantically scrabbling to afford another dose. Isabella borrowed against her future wages at the cafe, but even that became difficult, as her mother's growing weakness forced her to miss hours in order to care for her or for Abigail.

Mamma died when Isabella was twenty, and her fears of the past several years became indisputable fact. The sisters were alone in the world, and Isabella was the one who had to save them. But once she scraped together enough money to pay for Mamma's funeral, there was not a penny left to support them. She was in debt to her employer, and they would not give her anything more until she had paid off what she already owed. She could not find a second job, and even with the now-thirteen-year-old Abigail searching for work, Isabella knew they were not going to be able to make rent. They were scant weeks away from being evicted, and Isabella did not dare to think what would become of the Thorne sisters then. She sat awake at night, watching her sisters sleep, desperately trying to think of solutions that would not cost them their last scraps of dignity. But dignity, she decided, was cheap, at least compared to other concerns, like food and warmth and the desperate desire to avoid being forced into that oldest of professions to provide the basics for her family.

In desperation, Isabella wrote to one of Mamma's old friends in London, a woman named Mrs. Sheila Austin who had written to Mamma occasionally during her illness and even sent a little money for medicine when she could. Isabella had never met the woman, but she had little choice but to ask for help. She wrote to Mrs Austin to inform her of her mother's death, and, with a hollow stomach and shaking hand, added a line at the end mentioning the sisters' financial difficulty, and asking, in as polite a manner as she could muster, whether she might know of any family that would consider employing them as maids, or if she knew any other employment opportunity they might pursue.

Isabella posted the letter with very little hope of a response, let alone any actual help, and continued to sit awake at night, terrified of what the future would bring. So it was with no small amount of consternation that she received Mrs Austin's response a few days later, offering not condolences or a reference for a job, but Mrs Austin herself. The lady wrote that she would travel up from London as soon as she could manage it, and that she hoped that Miss Thorne would be kind enough to receive her. She had a proposal for her, she said, that could only be discussed in person.

CHAPTER 3

When she arrived, Mrs Austin turned out to be a short and somewhat round woman in her early fifties, with neatly arranged brown hair and a dress that seemed far too fine to belong in the Thorne sister's home. She sat carefully on one of the few chairs that they had to offer, and refused any offer of refreshment or tea.

"I was so very sorry to hear about your mother," she said, in the refined voice of a Londoner who was accustomed to far better society than those that could be found in a Liverpool slum. "She was a good woman."

"How did you know her?" Isabella asked. She took care to pronounce every word carefully, painfully aware of the difference in their accents.

"I lived in Liverpool once too," she said, "long ago. Before I met my husband. Business took us to London, but I recall caring for your mother as a child, and I was so happy to hear she married. And then, of course, the tragedy—"

"Yes," Isabella said, a little too abruptly to be polite. She did not like to think about her father's sudden death. Remembering how life had been before brought nothing but pain, and dwelling on past tragedy did nothing to remedy their current predicament. "It was a shock to all of us," she added, to smooth over her rudeness. "Mamma most of all."

Mrs Austin nodded. "And then for her to get sick as she did... well it was only natural, I suppose, with her heart broken and so much work to be done to support you girls. She would write to me, you know, and tell me how proud she was, of you in particular, Isabella. She said you were such a reliable, industrious girl. She could not have done without you."

"That's kind of you to say," Isabella said. She looked at Mrs Austin expectantly. Surely she had not come all this way simply to reminisce about her mother? Isabella had always thought that fine ladies were peculiar things, but that would be far too peculiar, taking the train a couple of hundred miles to visit when she had never taken such measures in all the time that Mamma was struggling and ill. But Isabella also got the sense that you could not challenge a lady like this to be more direct, that she would only speak when she was ready, and too much force would simply cause her to depart without offering any answers at all. So Isabella waited.

"You are probably wondering why I have come," Mrs Austin said, after another long pause. "It is something of a delicate situation, you understand, but your mother always said you were a good, sweet girl, and I may have a solution for your predicament, if you are willing."

"What kind of solution?" Isabella asked. Nerves squeezed her stomach. Mrs Austin almost sounded like she was about to ask Isabella to do something unsavoury, but surely a fine woman, and a friend of her mother's, would not have travelled all this way to make an offer that would bring the sisters' harm.

"My late husband, may God bless his soul, had a very good friend, a Mr Martin Kimble, here in Liverpool. Perhaps you have heard of him? He owns a shipping business, Kimble

Freighters, and is quite well-to-do. You may have seen the ships around the docks."

Isabella avoided the docks as much as she possibly could, after what happened to her father, but she simply nodded now, waiting for Mrs Austin to continue.

"Well, Mr Kimble sadly died several months ago, leaving the business and its fortune to his son, a Mr Daniel Kimble. He is a good man, hardworking and a kind soul, I believe, but he is unmarried, and his father always thought bachelorhood was bad for a young man. How could a man run a business such as Kimble Freighters, without a wife to help temper and guide him? As it turns out, Mr Kimble included a clause in his will, stating that he required his son to marry within a year of his death, or else the inheritance of the company would pass elsewhere."

"That is unfortunate," Isabella said carefully. "But what has this to do with me?"

"A marriage that lucrative," Mrs Austin said, "would set any girl up for life, regardless of her debts and the needs of her sisters. She could move to a comfortable house, and she would no longer have to work, except in supporting her husband, who would be a good man."

"You can't be suggesting that *I* should marry this Mr Kimble?" Isabella said, shocked.

"That is precisely what I am suggesting, my dear," Mrs Austin said.

Isabella shook her head. "If he is as rich and kind as you say, he could marry anyone he desired. He has time to find someone. Why would he ever wish to marry me, a strange girl from the slums? That cannot have been what his father intended."

"I doubt it was," Mrs Austin admitted. "But the younger Mr Kimble trusts me like an aunt, and he informed me of his problems himself. He does not know a single young lady that he should care to marry, and his mother is pushing him in a direction that he informs me he would very much wish to avoid."

"If he does not know a single person he could possibly bear to marry to save his inheritance," Isabella said, "then I doubt he will like me any better." If none of the sophisticated ladies of his acquaintance were adequate to his tastes, a girl like her, who had toiled cleaning blood off a butcher's shop floor and lived in a single room house with her sisters, would hardly tempt him.

"I believe that that is precisely why he will like you," Mrs Austin said. "His mother is always introducing him to the sort of girl she wishes he would marry, with wealth of their own and great interest in tea and silks and the latest fashions, but Mr Kimble finds all of it very shallow. He needs a wife with some brains and some stomach to her, someone with a strong spirit, and that, I believe, must surely describe you."

"But he does not know me," Isabella said. "And I do not know him."

"I understand," Mrs Austin said. "It would not be a love match, at least not at first. The man must marry someone, and he trusts my judgement. I wish to help you, my dear, and I think this will be a good opportunity for you. The man must marry, and you must turn about your fortunes. And you are due a gift of good luck, are you not, after all that has happened to you?"

Isabella considered this. She had never considered herself a romantic person. She did not lie awake at night, dreaming of falling in love. She had always been too busy worrying about more practical concerns. The idea of marriage had barely even occurred to her. She had too much to do, too many responsibilities, to go around falling in love. So she would not say that she was disappointed to imagine herself in a marriage of convenience, merely surprised. Such an arrangement must be entirely one-sided.

"I would be using him for his money," she said eventually. "If

I married him and did not love him. I would be gaining so much, and he would gain so little."

"That is not true, my dear," Mrs Austin said patiently. "He has much to gain from such a marriage. His entire inheritance, in fact. It would be to the benefit of both of you."

"But if his mother wishes him to marry someone with money and taste, like you say," Isabella said, "she will hardly approve of me, even if he does."

Mrs Austin waved her hand dismissively. "She is not the one who has to agree. And she merely wishes to see her son married and secure. She is a good woman, if a little set in her own opinions. Once she sees what a good girl you are, and once she sees her son happy and secure in his inheritance, she will be delighted with you, I am certain."

"And if Mr Kimble does not like me?" Isabella asked. It was a practical concern to have, after all, about such a practical arrangement. Mrs Austin's belief in her worthiness did not mean that Mr Kimble would agree, and she could not afford to waste time pursuing an engagement that would lead nowhere when the situation was so dire.

"If Mr Kimble does not like you, or you do not like him, then we need not take this any farther," Mrs Austin said. "But I believe that he will, and I believe you will like him too, well enough for this arrangement at least. With your permission, I could facilitate a meeting between the two of you? Then you can decide for yourself."

Isabella looked about the room, considering the situation. Part of it felt dishonest, a marriage for the sake of money on both sides. But was that not what rich people did all the time? They married for the convenience, for their business or their legacy, and cared little for the human side of it all. She would merely be doing the same, and securing both her family and this man's futures in the process. There was nothing so shameful about that. As long as he was not a brute – and even if he was, perhaps, if it meant keeping her sisters safe and fed….

"Yes," she said. "Please. I would like to meet him." A simple meeting could do no harm, after all. And perhaps this would be the answer she had been waiting for.

CHAPTER 4

Isabella met Mrs Austin and Mr Kimble for afternoon tea at a cafe in the nicer part of Liverpool the very next day. She put on her Sunday best dress and Tabitha helped her to arrange her hair in a way that suggested neatness and a little elegance, but Isabella still felt incredibly out of place as she stepped into the cafe. She felt shabby and unpolished, and she felt an unexpected rush of embarrassment and shame. But why should she be ashamed of who she was or where she came from, she thought, her old defiance striking in response. She had worked hard all her life to provide for her family, and if Mr Kimble or Mrs Austin looked down on her for that, *they* were the ones who should be ashamed. She was here on Mrs Austin's invitation, after all.

These thoughts, occurring so close together, meant that she had something of a stern, defiant expression on her face as she approached her mother's old friend and the stranger sitting beside her. To many, the expression would have been disconcerting, unsubtle and unladylike, but as Daniel Kimble watched her approach, he was simply struck by how strong and fearless she looked. She had the appearance of a maiden heading into battle, and the lack of delicacy piqued his interest at once. The girl was overly thin, but she had lush, thick dark hair, sharp, fierce eyes, and a small, sweetly shaped mouth. She looked like a young woman with personality, a girl who knew who she was and what she was about, and as Daniel Kimble rose to his feet, he thought that he liked her instantly.

Isabella, for her part, was less immediately struck by Mr Kimble's appearance, her heart locked away behind her defences and defiance. He was a handsome man, about thirty, tall with neat light brown hair and a slightly strong nose. Whether or not he was a good man would remain to be seen. Still, Isabella thought that her initial reservations had been proved true. A man such as this could easily find a wife, no matter how short the timeline required. It was strange that he would turn to Mrs Austin for help, and even stranger that an orphaned dockworker's daughter might meet his requirements where other, finer ladies had failed.

Still, Isabella was determined to be polite, as her mother had always taught her to be. When Mr Kimble rose to greet her, she bobbed into a curtsey, hoping she looked slightly more like a girl greeting a stranger at a ball, and less like a servant welcoming her master home. In truth, she looked like neither. Although Isabella could have pulled off the world's most theatrical curtsey if necessary, her confusion towards Mr Kimble meant that she did not look away from him, not even in the lowest point of her curtsey, making her greeting appear less like a sign of respect and more like a challenge.

"My dear Isabella," Mrs Austin said, sweeping forward and guiding her young charge towards a chair. "How good to see you again. Please allow me to introduce to you Mr Kimble, the son of one of my late husband's oldest friends. Mr Kimble, may I present to you Miss Thorne."

"It's a pleasure to meet you," Mr Kimble said.

"You too," Isabella said, hovering by the chair that Mrs Austin had indicated. Was she supposed to sit?

"Here," Mr Kimble said, "let me." He strode forward and pulled her chair out farther, indicating for her to sit. Feeling rather foolish, like a child playing at being a lady, Isabella sat, and Mr Kimble pushed her chair back in before taking his seat himself.

"Well," Mrs Austin said, once they were all seated. "Now that we are all acquainted. I believe you'll both get along splendidly."

"I believe so as well," Mr Kimble said with a smile, but Isabella could not bear this dance of politeness for another moment.

"I am certain I could get along well with you, sir," she said, "but I find myself at a loss as to why you would get along with me. If you don't mind my speaking bluntly,

sir—" and then she stopped, and reconsidered her words. She was supposed to be a potential *bride* for this man, was she not? Even if the idea was ridiculous, it seemed equally ridiculous that she should call him *sir* and not his name. If he did not like her addressing him as such, then the marriage would never work anyway. "Mr Kimble, I mean," she said, reaching into her knowledge of how the finer ladies talked at the cafe as she served them. "Mr Kimble, you are clearly a man of some means. You strike me as well-mannered and more than handsome enough, and I am certain Mrs Austin's faith in you does you credit as well. If I may speak bluntly, Mr Kimble, I do not see a single reason why you would struggle to find a wife, especially if you are so desperate as to consider marrying a poor stranger such as me. Mrs Austin has kindly explained the situation to me and invited me here, but I am utterly perplexed as to why you would agree."

Mr Kimble, for his part, smiled. Isabella spoke quickly and bluntly, her eyes fierce like a warrior's despite the polite turn of her words, and he was struck, once again, by how unlike any of the women his mother had attempted to set him up with she was. They were all too concerned with the idea of his fortune and the rules of politeness to express a single challenging thought in his presence, and the result was boredom on both sides.

"Miss Thorne," he said. "You say that our friend Mrs Austin's faith in me does me credit, but you forget that her faith in *you* must then give you credit as well. My mother has recommended many women to me to help solve my practical dilemma, and I could not imagine even a tolerable level of happiness with any of them. Mrs Austin has recommended only one young woman to me, and that young woman is you. Don't you think that single recommendation is worth consideration?"

"Perhaps that is so," Isabella said, raising her chin slightly, "but I admit I find myself confused by Mrs Austin's recommendation too. I trust you are aware of my background?"

"Mrs Austin told me some," he said. "How you tragically lost your father as a child, and worked to support your mother and two sisters. How you recently lost your mother to a long and sad illness, and find yourself struggling to continue on. How could I not feel sympathy?"

"Am I a charity case to you, then, Mr Kimble?"

"No," Mr Kimble said. "But I believe we are both looking for opportunities, and if we work together, we can both be happy. I do not wish to marry any of the women my mother is foisting upon me. I could not be happy in such a marriage, and I doubt they would be either. I have my work to focus on, and I am not a great romantic. You need a safe place for you and your sisters to live, to ease your worries. I believe we will make a valuable pair."

"Are you proposing a business arrangement, then, Mr Kimble?" Isabella asked.

"Yes," he said. "I suppose I am."

Isabella bit her lip. "If I agree," she said, after a moment, "how am I to know this is not some evil scheme? That my sisters and I will not be locked in the cellar or some such, once you have your inheritance and our usefulness is over?"

"Isabella!" Mrs Austin cried, but Mr Kimble only chuckled.

"A fan of the Gothic, are you, Miss Thorne?"

"The novels, Mr Kimble? I can hardly read, growing up as I did. And if I could, when would I have time for novels? Dramatic things might happen in stories, Mr Kimble, but they happen in real life too, to unsuspecting women of all kinds. We sign away everything about ourselves when we marry, and we can only pray our husbands will treat us kindly."

He nodded in concession. "That may be so, Miss Thorne, but I can assure you I have no such designs. If I were looking for a damsel, my mother has thrown several my way. What I want, Miss Thorne, is to receive my inheritance, appease my mother and my late father by taking a wife that she can fuss over if she wishes, and to not be concerned that I am disappointing my wife by not being the sort of domestic man that I am decidedly not. If what you want is a husband who will keep you and your sisters safe and otherwise not interfere with your lives too greatly, then I believe we will make a splendid deal."

"And if you later decide you don't like me?"

"Impossible," Mr Kimble said. "I already like you tremendously, Miss Thorne. I find it hard to imagine anyone who might dislike you."

The compliment was a warm one, but Isabella could not be deterred. "That does not answer my question," she said. "You have known me for all of five minutes, and I have been near arguing with you this entire time. How am I to know what you will feel after an hour, or a week, or a year?"

"I can promise never to be cruel to you," Mr Kimble said. "And if you decide that you do not like *me*, then you may leave my house to live apart whenever you wish, and I will ensure you have funds enough to keep you. I appreciate my duties as a husband, Miss Thorne."

"And if I do agree?" she asked.

"Then you and your sisters will move into my home with me here in the city after the wedding. I have some servants, Miss Thorne, which would require some management, and when I entertain other businessmen, it would be a boon to have my wife beside me. Otherwise, you may do as you wish. I have been building quite a sizeable library, if that intrigues you. Perhaps you could work on your reading and finally find time for some more *fictional* dastardly tales."

"I see, Mr Kimble," Isabella said, with a mischievous turn of her lips. "So you are the one with a fondness for the Gothic."

"I read very dull reports about shipping all day, Miss Thorne," he replied. "A man needs his entertainment in the evening as well."

Isabella looked him up and down again, considering. She knew she was not particularly in a position to be choosy or disagreeable, when her entire family's wellbeing was at stake. But all of her comments and questions had been necessary, she thought. She could not risk saving her sisters from one dire situation and immediately forcing them into a worse one. It was her job to look out for them, in every way she could. Isabella found she trusted Mrs Austin's judgement, and she trusted the words that Mr Kimble spoke. She may not be about to embark on a great romance with this man, but she could not turn her nose up at security, and so far, this appeared a far more luxurious form of security than she had ever dreamed of. It would be no difficulty to be married to such a well-spoken, determined sort of man, she thought, even if just for convenience. Especially if just for convenience, for then there would be no pressure on either of them to be anything more than they actually were.

"Very well, Mr Kimble," she said, after a long moment. "We

are in agreement, I believe." She stuck out her hand, and he took it, shaking it firmly.

"It is a pleasure to be working with you," Mr Kimble said, with an ironic little smile.

"And you as well, Mr Kimble," Isabella replied. "I am certain this will prove an excellent partnership."

CHAPTER 5

"Tell me what he looks like again," Abigail said that evening, when the three sisters gathered at home to discuss the day's events. "I can't believe that he's young and handsome. I'd bet a man looking for a marriage like this would be an old gargoyle, any day of the week."

Isabella laughed. "You mustn't say that in front of him," she said to her twelve-year-old sister. "I doubt he'd appreciate it."

"Even if we're saying that he's *not* a gargoyle?" Abigail asked. "He'd prefer that, wouldn't he? Men are strange, but they're not *that* strange."

"It sounds to me," Tabitha said, "that you almost said the same thing to him yourself, Izzy. Accusing him of planning to lock us all in a cellar!"

"I did not accuse him," Isabella said, giving her sister a little shove. "But a girl has to ask."

"I doubt that's in any of the novels," Tabitha said. "I love you, but by the way, are you planning to turn into a villain and torture me for the rest of my days?"

"Well, maybe it should be," Isabella said. "It might save them a lot of trouble. And how would you know anyway? You've never read a novel in your life."

"No," Tabitha said, "but maybe I will, now that you're going to be marrying Mr Rich and Handsome."

"I never said he was handsome," Isabella said.

"You implied it," Abigail replied.

"Heavily implied it," Tabitha added. She flopped back onto the bed that the three sisters shared, her dark hair fanning around her face. "I think it's terribly romantic."

"You think it's romantic?" Isabella repeated, poking her sister with her foot. Her big toe was beginning to poke through her stockings. She really needed to darn them soon. "Everything about this is the exact opposite of romantic. He never even proposed, Tabs. We shook hands to agree to it."

"*Much* more romantic than a traditional proposal," Tabitha insisted. "You'll pretend it's a business arrangement, but you'll fall for each other, and it will be wonderful. And then perhaps he has some handsome young friends too, for me and Abigail."

"I don't want to marry any of his friends," Abigail said, "handsome or not."

"Then what do you intend to do?" Isabella asked her.

"I haven't decided yet," Abigail said primly. "Whatever it is, it's going to be excellent."

"When do you meet his family?" Tabitha asked, sitting up again.

"He doesn't have much," Isabella said. "Just his mother, I think, and she's visiting friends down south in Brighton or somewhere."

"Where's Brighton?" Abigail asked.

"Down south," Tabitha replied, in a *don't be stupid* sort of voice. "By the sea, but a nice sea. It's on the beach."

"Maybe we'll get to go to Brighton," Abigail said wistfully. "After Izzy is married."

"Maybe," Isabella agreed, although at that moment she could

not really imagine that far ahead. She felt like she had spent her whole life simply hanging on until tomorrow. To imagine leisure like that in the future seemed guaranteed to chase the possibility away. "We can worry about that later."

"I'm not worried!" Abigail said. "It's exciting."

"Well, if you want it to happen," Isabella said, "we all have to be on our best behaviour, *especially* when we finally meet his mother. She won't be back in Liverpool until after the wedding, but we still need to get on her good side. We all need to act like father would have wished us to, not like girls who grew up in the slums."

"We can do both," Abigail said. "And he knows who we are. I thought that's why he wanted you."

"Knowing it and seeing it are two different things," Isabella said. "So be good, the both of you."

"We always are," Tabitha said, which was a lie if Isabella had ever heard one. But instead of arguing, she simply reached out and stroked her sister's hair.

"I know," Isabella said softly. "And things will be all right now. You'll see."

ISABELLA DID NOT SEE Daniel Kimble again until the day they were married. Mrs Austin remained in Liverpool, as an aide and a witness to the event, and she helped Isabella with all the preparations that were required. These were not numerous, as both Isabella and Mr Kimble were eager to see the marriage arranged as swiftly as possible. Isabella initially imagined marrying in her Sunday best, but Mrs Austin would not hear of such a thing, and she had Isabella measured for a far finer and more fashionable dress. The dress could not be stored at the sisters' abode, as it was almost white, inspired by the example set by the queen herself, and simply being in the air of the sisters' neighbourhood would stain the cloth. Although the cut was fairly simple, with minimal silk and no lace, it was the most beautiful garment that Isabella had ever seen, let alone owned. Her sisters helped her to dress in it the morning of her wedding, and Isabella was frightened even to breathe, in case the movement somehow damaged the cloth.

Mrs Austin lent Isabella her own old veil, as all of her mother's wedding things had been sold or lost long ago. Isabella had no wedding chest to bring with her, nothing to contribute to her marriage except for her sisters and herself, but she could not help feeling hope as she considered herself in the looking glass. She had never had time to consider whether or not she was beautiful, and the truth either way hardly mattered considering the reason for her marriage, but she could not help thinking that she looked handsome in the dress, with her hair pinned just so by her sisters and a veil fixed to the crown of her head. She was a little pale with nerves, but her eyes were bright, and she could see the effect of this new sense of hope on her complexion. After today, she and her sisters would not have to worry about money or food. She could get her sisters away from the bad air of the slums that had poisoned their mother. And even if she did not love Mr Kimble, and he did not love her, she felt certain their lives would all be better once the vows had been spoken.

If the vicar saw anything strange about a well-to-do man marrying a slightly rough-mannered girl before the minimum number of witnesses, he did not comment on it. He intoned his way through the ceremony with all the solemnity that such an occasion required, and Isabella and Mr Kimble both said their piece when the script required. It was, Isabella considered, rather like playing a part on stage, as she liked to do as a child. She spoke her lines, and smiled when a maiden might be expected to smile, keeping her eyes on her hands. When the vicar declared them man and wife and Mr Kimble pulled back her veil, she was struck again by how tall he was, and the kindness in his face as he bent to kiss her. Isabella accepted his kiss with only a slight tilt upwards of her own head, and she was surprised how warm his lips felt as they brushed against hers. Her heart leapt slightly as he moved away, and she found herself smiling, genuinely this time, as her eyes met his. She was not a fool, to believe there was anything more between them than convenience, but for that moment, she felt a kind of calm and warmth she had not felt since her mother fell ill, or perhaps even longer, since before her father had died.

CHAPTER 6

The three sisters moved out of their house in the slums and into Mr Kimble's townhouse, which had room for all of them and more besides. Abigail was so excited by the sight of a bedroom all her own that she spun around it in circles with her arms outstretched, laughing, before collapsing on the plush mattress of the bed. The servants looked askance at the sisters, with their slightly rough accents and their lack of understanding of some of the rules of society, but they never commented on the situation out loud, and Isabella decided that was enough to satisfy her. She would win them over with time, she knew, and she set out trying to be as good a mistress of the house as anyone could hope for. She had sense enough of reading and accounting after working in the cafe for so many years, and she exerted herself to learn more, spending many hours in Mr Kimble's library and asking questions of everyone she could. She practiced her accent too, taking to her new position like a grand role on stage, with the hope that one day, the role of Mrs Kimble would come as naturally to her as being Miss Isabella Thorne.

Her initial wariness of feeling towards Daniel faded as she

settled into the house. He still gave her that ironic little smile when she made errors of etiquette, but he seemed delighted by both her manner and her opinions, and he often returned from a day's work with a new fascinating book that he was certain would excite her. Some of these were educational, but many others were novels and poems, and the new couple would read them together by the firelight in the evenings and debate their characters and their merits until exhaustion won out and they retired to bed. Isabella found particular joy in reading the new volumes from a Yorkshire author, titled *Jane Eyre*, which made her think that perhaps courage and determination would win out after all. Daniel, for his part, was more one for the Romantic poets, his calm businessman's exterior concealing a great love of melodrama, and soon Isabella found herself teasing him about his tastes, describing her feelings about breakfast or the cloudy weather like a poet in the throes of agony, and eliciting his much treasured laugh.

Abigail was able to focus on schooling, while Tabitha insisted on taking over Isabella's position at the cafe, a lifetime's experience telling her to work hard and save whatever she could in case of future disaster. Isabella could not fault her cautiousness, and the work seemed to give her sister pleasure, despite the temper of the cafe owner. In a few short weeks, all three sisters were looking brighter and healthier, their hearts buoyed by the new life they found themselves in. The only great pain was the still recent loss of their Mamma, and sometimes the girls would gather in Abigail's room, with their blankets wrapped around them, and remember her through tears and laughter.

Isabella knew that all her good fortune could collapse at any moment, as it had before, but the weeks brought a sense of ease to her life that she had all but forgotten, and she began to trust that perhaps things would work out after all. The only point of difficulty came when Daniel invited his business associates over for dinner. As mistress of the house and Daniel's blushing new bride, Isabella was expected to welcome the gentlemen and their wives and charm them with her own wit and elegance and grace. But when the businessmen appeared, Isabella felt she had none of these traits. The chatter that so delighted Daniel when they were alone seemed too loud and brash around others, and whenever she interjected herself into conversation, people fell silent around her, judging her for some faux pas she could not quite identify. She felt out of place, an embarrassment, and was determined to study up for the role and make sure she fulfilled her part of the marriage bargain. But when Isabella broached the topic with her husband, he simply laughed the problem away. He liked her just as she was, he said, and his stuffy business associates could use a little more liveliness in their days.

Isabella assumed that her husband had written to inform his mother of the wedding, and that her new mother-in-law had chosen not to return, perhaps out of frustration at his defiance. She worried about the first meeting, which most inevitably would one day occur, but Daniel dismissed that concern too, telling her that his mother could hardly be anything else than charmed by her, and Isabella tried her hardest to believe him.

It was early evening, a couple of months after the wedding, when Isabella heard a fierce pounding on the townhouse's front door. Daniel had yet to return from a day's work, and the servants were all busy working on preparing supper, so Isabella rose to answer it herself.

"No, don't concern yourself about it, Agnes," she said to the maid, who appeared at the top of the stairs. "I'll deal with it."

Agnes bobbed into a curtsey and vanished again.

When Isabella opened the door, she was almost immediately knocked back by the force of the visitor who pushed her way inside. She was a tall woman, in her fifties, dressed in mourning, with her grey-blonde hair pulled in a bun beneath a black hat. She was birdlike in appearance, with a long nose and narrow cheeks, but her manner was more that of a bull. "Where is he?" she snapped, without a moment's introduction. "Where is my son?"

"Mrs Kimble," Isabella guessed, taking a slight step back. "He isn't home yet."

"And who are you?" Mrs Kimble asked, looking Isabella up and down with narrow eyes.

"My name is Isabella, ma'am," she said, the deferential term slipping out under the force of Mrs Kimble's glare. "Mrs Isabella Kimble. I am your son's new wife."

"New wife?" Mrs Kimble repeated. "What nonsense. My son has excellent marriage prospects, and I can assure you, you are not among them."

"I don't know what to tell you, ma'am," Isabella said. "I can promise you, we are married, and have been since two months back. I thought he had informed you."

"Why would he inform me," Mrs Kimble asked, "when clearly he cares so little for his mother's opinion? I heard a rumour in Brighton that he had married, and I came here as soon as I could to confirm that it was untrue."

"I'm afraid it is true, ma'am," Isabella said. "I am sorry that he did not inform you—"

Daniel chose that moment to return. "Mother!" he said, as he stepped down from the cab. "You've returned."

Mrs Kimble immediately turned on him, shutting Isabella out entirely. "Daniel. What is this I am hearing about you being *married*?"

"It's true, Mother," Daniel said. He strode up to the door and clapped his hand on Isabella's arm. "Aren't you pleased for me? I found true love and respectability after all. May I present your new daughter-in-law, Mrs Isabella Kimble."

"Daniel," Mrs Kimble said, and her voice wavered slightly. "You truly got married without inviting your mother?" The slight tremble in her tone struck Isabella's heart. She would have given almost anything to have her mamma alive and able to attend her wedding, and she could hardly imagine one day having a son of her own, raising him and loving him so, and then being left out of something so significant, simply because she happened to be vacationing a little far away.

"I'm very sorry, Mrs Kimble," Isabella said. "We did not mean to exclude you—"

"I am talking to my son," Mrs Kimble snapped, and Isabella took a slight step back from the force of the vitriol in Mrs Kimble's voice.

"Isabella," Daniel said, "perhaps you should wait in the library."

Isabella opened her lips to argue, but stopped herself before she could speak. Daniel knew his mother far better than she did. He would know how to appease her. This was one moment where she simply had to play the role of his perfect wife, and she got the sense that she had already erred somehow.

"All right," she said, after a moment. "If you'll excuse me, Mrs Kimble."

She walked away with as much dignity and poise as she could muster, and closed the library door behind her with a resounding click. But the walls of the house were too thin to block out the hissed conversation that echoed from the hallway.

"Her *accent*, Daniel. Where did you find her, the dockyard?"

"Isabella has had a rough start in life," Daniel said, "but she is everything I could have wanted in a wife. Mrs Austin introduced us."

"Mrs Austin!" his mother laughed. "There's a woman who rose too far above her station too, I'd wager. To think you would shove dear Clare aside for such a girl."

"I never shoved dear Clare aside, Mother. I never considered her. You were the one pursuing that match."

"Clare is an excellent young woman. She has a good family,

and her father's business complements ours so well. It was an ideal match—"

"An ideal match, except for the fact that I did not want to marry her."

"It cannot be too late," his mother replied. Their voices grew quieter, as though Daniel were steering them into another room. "I am certain we can find a reason for an annulment—"

"That's enough, Mother," Daniel said. "I am married. It is done."

Isabella sank into one of the library chairs as the voices faded. She had not necessarily expected Daniel's mother to embrace her on their first meeting, but she was shaken by the force of her distaste. She should not have answered the door herself, she thought. That was her first misstep. But it could not be helped. She would have to simply try harder to win the woman's approval. She must have been in shock, to find her son had married without informing her. It would take a little time for Isabella to win her over, but Isabella was accustomed to hard work.

Isabella saw Mrs Kimble again just before the woman departed the house for the evening. This time, Mrs Kimble embraced Isabella, pressing a kiss to her cheek as she moved away, as though her son's words had moved her after all. But Isabella saw the sharpness that remained in the older woman's eyes as she considered her. There was no real warmth in that expression, and Isabella felt, with dark certainty, that the animosity from her new mother-in-law was far from over.

CHAPTER 7

*I*sabella met the famous Clare several days later, when she and Daniel were invited over to Mrs Kimble's for afternoon tea. Miss Clare Swindon was a sweet looking young woman, the quintessential English rose of beauty, with smooth white skin and golden blonde locks. Her cheeks glowed the pink of either a healthy blush or some perfectly applied rouge, and her movements seemed to flow.

"Daniel," she said, upon seeing him, as she rose to offer him her hand. Even Isabella, as unpractised in society as she was, saw the inappropriateness of an unmarried young woman calling her husband by his Christian name, but she forced herself to smile politely and wait for her introduction.

"May I please call you Isabella?" Miss Swindon said, once Isabella was introduced. "And you must call me Clare. I am certain we will be the best of friends. I have known Daniel for years, you know. I can tell you all the stories that will make him blush."

Although her words were friendly, there was a decisive gleam in her eyes that set Isabella on edge, even as Clare leaned forward and pressed a kiss to each of Isabella's cheeks.

"You must tell me all about yourself," Miss Swindon said, as she settled back in her seat and beckoned for Isabella to sit beside her.

"Yes," Mrs Kimble said, a little drily. "We are eager to know."

"How did you meet Daniel?" Clare asked. "He kept you such a secret. He has never mentioned you, at least to my hearing."

Isabella glanced at Daniel. "A family friend introduced us," she said, after a moment. "Do you know Mrs Austin?"

"I can't say I've had the pleasure," Miss Swindon said.

"She's an old acquaintance of my late husband," Mrs Kimble said. "A highly interesting woman." The way Mrs Kimble said it, Isabella knew that *interesting* was not a compliment.

"Oh, we simply must have everyone around at my father's for dinner one evening," Miss Swindon said. "Say you will come, Isabella! How fun it will be. We have just acquired a new pianoforte too— do you play, Isabella?"

Isabella was forced to admit that she did not.

"That is a pity," Miss Swindon said. "Of course, my mother simply insisted I started learning as soon as I could walk. I wish I were more accomplished at it, but I suppose my talents will have to suffice for an evening."

"Don't be silly, Clare, dear," Mrs Kimble said. "You play so beautifully. I am sure everyone will be enraptured. Does she not play beautifully, Daniel?"

"I am no expert on music," Daniel said politely, "but if you believe so, Mother, it must be true."

"And surely you must play whist, Isabella. We have such fun with our games."

Isabella again admitted that she did not.

"Well, we shall teach you," Miss Swindon said. "Will we not, Mrs Kimble? It shall be a wonderful time. I have already decided."

Isabella folded her hands carefully in her lap and tried to pretend that she was not blushing. Clare was effusive in her welcomes, but Isabella could sense the disdain wrapped in every word, the subtle implication that Isabella was not good enough to be in their company.

And Isabella supposed she was right. A few weeks ago, she had been living in a one room house in the slums with her sisters. She had earned a living serving ladies like Miss Clare Swindon and Mrs Kimble. She did not fit here, despite how hard she tried to play the role. But if she could not change her past, she thought, she could at least change her manners now.

"There," Daniel said, as they travelled home from his mother's. "That went much better."

"Your mother doesn't like me," Isabella said softly. "And Miss Swindon doesn't either."

"Oh, she's a bit stuck up," Daniel admitted. "Why do you think I didn't want to marry her? So prim, don't you think? But I'm certain she means well."

Isabella was not so convinced, but she did not want to argue. Daniel knew his mother and Miss Swindon better than she did, and she would have to trust him. Still, as soon as they returned home, she retired to the study and experimentally pressed some of the keys on the pianoforte. After a long moment, Daniel followed her.

"Do you know how to play?" she asked him.

"A little," he said. "Never well enough to appease my mother."

"Will you teach me?"

"Are you worrying about what Clare said?" He sat down on the piano stool beside her. "Isabella, I like you exactly as you are. *You* are the wife I chose. I didn't want a pretentious housewife like her. I wanted *you*."

The words warmed Isabella, but they could not entirely erase her doubt. "Still," she said. "I want to learn."

"Then I can teach you," Daniel said, putting one hand gently over hers on the keys. "If you would like."

∽

Isabella soon learned everything Daniel could teach her about the piano and more beside. Playing reminded her of being a child, inventing songs with her friends in the street, running home and singing them to her Mamma and Papa. She learned to read sheet music, but she found the most joy simply pressing the keys herself, listening to the notes ring and beginning to weave them together into tunes of her own. She would hum to herself as she did, the music reverberating inside her, long-forgotten memories awakening with every sound.

She was grateful for the solace this new talent offered, because although Mrs Kimble and Miss Swindon continued to be polite when Daniel was present, their sharp looks and deftly veiled insults left it plain how they really felt about Isabella. Isabella, for her part, tried to please them by working on her accent and her word choice, by engaging with them in conversation about the things that they seemed to love, even by attempting to speak with Miss Swindon about music and the piano, but she could sense, with skills honed by years of needing to understand others' emotions to survive, that they despised her.

And the distaste towards her did not end with Daniel's family. He would bring business associates home for dinner or entertainment at least once a week now, and every time, Isabella could not help feeling awkward and out of place. None of their guests ever said anything to her directly, but she could see the glances shared between husbands and wives when she made some slight social faux pas, or the way people's faces would tighten sometimes with disapproval. Every time Isabella saw this, she would try to think what error she had made, so she would not make it again, but she was not always certain, and when she asked Daniel about it, he simply laughed it away. She made dinners far more interesting, he told her, than anyone else, and the way he said *interesting* made it a clear compliment not an insult.

"My dear," Daniel said, after she confessed her fears to him one night, and the endearment filled her with warmth. "I just want you to be yourself." He took her hands in his, squeezing them gently. "*You* are my wife, not Clare Swindon or anyone else my mother might want you to be. You are perfect the way you are."

She smiled softly, but she could not believe him. "But your business associates—" she said.

"I want my business associates to meet *you*, Isabella. Just you. They will love you exactly as you are, just as I do. And if they don't, then they'll have to answer to me, all right?"

But Isabella could not see how that could be true. They had both been clear that this marriage was one of convenience, and that meant she needed to play the role of a good wife perfectly. That was, she thought, how she would earn her place here and repay Daniel for all his kindness and support.

"You needed to get married because of your business," she said slowly. "You cannot alienate your father's associates."

"I do not intend to," Daniel said. "I intend to continue the business as my own, and have the wife I chose beside me. Don't give it any more space in your thoughts, Isabella. You are worth a hundred of any of them."

When Daniel spoke to her like that, Isabella found it far too easy to forget the initial purpose of their union. She treasured every moment she got to spend alone with Daniel, and sometimes she dared to think that perhaps he treasured them too. He had a dry sort of humour that had been a little difficult to get used to, but after a time, Isabella found herself teasing him back, and that always elicited a smile. He was intelligent and kind, and he always had interesting things to say about the new books he acquired that they read together, but Isabella was discovering there was something more to him as well, something indefinable beneath the surface, a spark that glowed seemingly only for her. Was this, she wondered, what love was?

It is a business arrangement, she would tell herself, in the dark of the night, when her hopes burned too brightly, Daniel fast asleep beside her. *It was a practical decision for us both.* But she could not deny the warmth that grew in her heart, and she could not quiet the voice that said Daniel felt the same for her. Every time he insisted that he wanted her to be herself, to be Isabella Kimble, every time he laughed at one of her comments or praised her musical education to his business associates, every time he brought home a book he thought would interest her or kissed her cheek as he passed her, while she read in an armchair, her heart fluttered with the feeling that perhaps he cared for her too.

And if his mother could not love her, she also could not undo what had been done and end the marriage against her son's wishes. She seemed to tolerate Isabella's presence, and Isabella could only hope that, as she saw her son's happiness in his marriage, she would grow to appreciate her new daughter-in-law, even if she could not love her.

So when Isabella received an invitation from Mrs Kimble one Saturday afternoon for Isabella and her sisters to accompany her to visit one of her oldest friends, Isabella felt that flutter of hope that things might be improving again. Mrs Kimble had never sought out Isabella's company alone, merely endured it in order to see her son, and an invitation not only to spend some time with her and her sisters, but to be introduced to others in Mrs Kimble's social circle, must surely mean she was warming to Isabella, or at least attempting so. Isabella smiled as she dressed in her finest blue day-dress, listening fondly to her sisters' chatter as she pinned her hair up into a neat, respectable bun.

Mrs Kimble met them in a carriage, and they rode along the bumpy road together in silence at first, Isabella struggling to think what to say. After inquiring after Mrs Kimble's health and commenting on the fair weather, Isabella let the silence lapse around them. Why had Mrs Kimble invited them, if she did not wish to speak?

Yet when they arrived at the home of Mrs Kimble's friend, Mrs Kimble herself became far warmer than Isabella had ever known her. She introduced the three sisters as her new daughters, and smiled as she told her friend about the improvements her son had made to the townhouse and how promising his business prospects looked now that he had a wife beside him. The three sisters remained as quiet as was polite during the afternoon, not wishing to make any error of etiquette that might disrupt this new-found calm, but as Abigail was coaxed into talking about her schooling and her new study of the French language, Isabella could not help but smile. She had made the right choice in her marriage, she knew. Somehow, God had seen her struggles and blessed her with the perfect husband, arriving in such an unexpected way. And if Mrs Kimble was now accepting them, as she seemed to be, then her younger sisters would have all the opportunities that Isabella herself had not had. They would be able to move in good society, and make good marriages of their own, and maybe even have a mother figure in their lives after Mamma's tragic passing.

It was with a light heart that Isabella walked home with her sisters and Mrs Kimble, the latter telling the coachman to trail them in case he was needed but insisting that they should not waste a beautiful afternoon inside carriage walls. Again, she said little as they walked, but Isabella decided that perhaps this was a good sign too. Mrs Kimble was not taking the opportunity to berate or correct her. It was a companionable silence, she thought, and that was progress too.

Mrs Kimble bid the sisters farewell with a kiss on the cheek for each of them, and they waited on the doorstep to wave as Mrs Kimble stepped into the carriage and departed. As soon as they stepped inside, Isabella's sisters both scurried away, Abigail to write about events in her new diary and Tabitha to practice on the pianoforte herself, after learning from her sister, and Isabella went in search of her husband. He was not in the study or the parlour, and Isabella climbed the stairs carefully, wondering where he might be.

Perhaps, she told herself, he had felt the house too quiet with all the sisters gone, and went to meet a friend of his own. Isabella had to fight back a smile at the thought of her husband looking lost in the middle of the echoing townhouse, unsure how to entertain himself without the Thorne sisters causing chaos around him.

The door to the bedroom was ajar, but Isabella did not think much of it as she walked along the landing, fiddling with her earrings as she went. She would change into something more comfortable than the clothes required for appeasing her new mother-in-law, and then read a little more until Daniel returned.

The door creaked as she pushed it open, and it took her a moment to understand what she was seeing in the dim light beyond. The curtains had been drawn – strange, she thought vaguely, for the sun was not unbearably bright today and it was still only late afternoon – and the bedclothes were all in a tumble, despite Isabella having personally tidied them just that morning. In fact, they were not merely messy but uneven and lumpy, as though someone slept beneath them.

"Daniel?" she said softly as she stepped farther into the gloom. "Are you unwell?"

She could see an arm on top of the bedclothes, and as her eyes adjusted to the dark, she realised, to her dawning horror, that there were two figures lying there beneath the sheets, two people asleep in her bed, a larger one and a smaller one. Her stomach dropped. Isabella marched over to the window and yanked open the drapes, letting the sunlight reveal the scene before her.

Daniel was asleep on his side of the bed, his face pressed into his pillow. From the little that Isabella could see of his shoulders, he was not even wearing a nightshirt. And another figure stirred beside him. A messy head of light blonde hair sat up, the sheets wrapped around her, and Isabella found herself looking into the bright blue eyes of Clare Swindon.

CHAPTER 8

Clare did not look surprised to see her. She blinked sleepily at Isabella, and then her face was lit with the beginnings of a smile. Daniel still did not stir.

But that was for the best, Isabella thought, through the panic and anger now pounding in her ears. She could not bear to hear his voice. She took in the tableau, and she knew that her heart could deny the truth no longer. Her husband had betrayed her. He had never seen her as anything more than a useful business tool, and even that usefulness had not been enough to inspire him to faithfulness and keep Clare Swindon from his bed. *Clare Swindon*, a woman he claimed to dislike, the woman who constantly made Isabella feel inadequate but who Daniel always insisted was Isabella's inferior, the woman whose manners and charms were always so perfect and who had caused Isabella to *beg* her husband to help her improve her own.

All this time, her husband had been laughing at her. He had been praising her to her face, and then as soon as she looked away, he had been insulting her in her own bed. How often had Clare come here, she wondered. And was it only Clare? Or did her husband have several *eligible women* to consort with outside of his poor, coarse, stupid wife?

It took mere seconds for all of this to run through Isabella's head. In that time, Clare Swindon made no move to hide or apologise. Isabella met her gaze, and then nodded once, half to Clare and half to herself. She grabbed a bag from the closet and swept up the few possessions she had brought to the house. Apart from the clothes on her back, she took nothing that Daniel had given her since her arrival, nothing that her supposed marriage had earned her. Then she strode downstairs, still with no one following her, to find her sisters.

"Pack up your things," she said, and she was surprised by how steady her voice was. "We're leaving."

"Leaving?" Tabitha asked. "Dear Izzy, what's the matter?"

"Later," Isabella said. "We will talk about it later. But we are leaving now." If she paused to say what she had seen aloud, she worried she would collapse from the weight of it, and she could not let that happen. She and her sisters were not beggars, they were not charity cases, and they were not to be laughing stocks. They must depart at once.

And depart they did. Isabella did not allow her gaze to linger on the books or the pianoforte as she closed the study door. She hurried her sisters and their possessions out of the front door and immediately went to hail a cab. She did not quite know where she was going. She only understood that she could not remain here for another minute. Not in this house, and not in this city, that had stolen so much from her and her family and that mocked her now. She instructed the cab driver to take them to Liverpool Station, and she ignored her sisters' entreaties for an explanation as the horse pulled them on their way through the busy, cobbled streets.

The weather no longer seemed beautiful. The warmth of the sun was mocking her, she thought, as she climbed out of the cab and handed a couple of coins to the driver. Her sisters asked again where they were going as Isabella strode towards the station, and all Isabella could think was that they must go *away*, far from here.

"We will visit Mrs Austin," Isabella said, not even realising that was her plan until she had spoken it aloud. "In London. Come on. I will enquire about the next train."

"Mrs Austin?" Abigail asked. She ran after her eldest sister, her case of scant possessions banging against her leg. "Why?"

"I should like to see her," Isabella said. She had slipped into the most pretentious way of speaking, the one she tried to use around Mrs Kimble and Daniel's business associates, and that stung too, because she never performed that role well enough, did she? She had failed, and yet here she was, still trying to act like the rich businessman's wife, even around her own sisters. Still, she succeeded in purchasing tickets on the next train to London, which departed in two hours' time, and then settled with her sisters in the waiting room. With shaking hands, she scribbled a note to Mrs Austin, uncertain if it could possibly arrive before they did – it might even be carried on the same train they now held tickets for – and posted it. Once that was done, she felt a little calmer, a little firmer, knowing that she had acted in the only way she really could.

Then she let out a breath and looked around the waiting room. It was quiet apart from the sisters, who were now looking at her with concern. "Mr Kimble has insulted me," she said eventually. "Our marriage is over. We cannot accept another penny from him or his family."

"Oh, Izzy," Tabitha said. She wrapped her arms around her sister, and Isabella leaned into her.

"Insulted you?" repeated Abigail, who was still only twelve. "What do you mean?"

"He loves another woman," Tabitha said, in a low voice, "when he should only love our Izzy."

Abigail looked immediately furious. "Why would anyone

want anyone else, if they could have our Izzy? He's a fool, Isabella. We don't need him."

"No," Isabella said softly. "We don't."

Abigail seemed to think for a moment. "I could go back there and kick him for you, if you like. If he deserves it."

"He definitely deserves it," Tabitha said, "but we have a train to catch. But we will do something, Isabella, once we get to London. We will. We will write to all of his business associates and their wives and tell them what he has done. He will see if he is so popular and successful then."

But Isabella shook her head. What was the merit in fighting like that? She had been the fool here, to trust a stranger like Daniel, to read more into the situation than actually existed. She did not want to increase the sting and infamy of the insult, by informing others. Even telling Mrs Austin would be more pain and embarrassment than she wished to suffer. The best thing, the *only* thing, she could do was depart, as quickly as she could.

The sun set around them as the train pulled its way through the English countryside, leaving the brick and smoke of Liverpool behind. None of the girls had ever ridden on a train before, but Isabella was too wretched and Tabitha too worried about her sister to enjoy it. Abigail seemed deeply concerned too, but she could not resist looking out of the window and listening to the rhythmic clicking and rattling of the wheels beneath them.

Isabella stared out of the window too, her hands clutched tightly around her bag. Her wedding ring felt too tight and heavy on her finger, but she refused to remove it. Not yet, at least. She was a married woman, for all that it helped her now. She listened to the sounds of the train hurtling south, and tried not to think about the scene she had left, the city she was travelling to or the one she was leaving behind.

It was late by the time they arrived in London, and the three sisters clung to their bags as they made their way through the station, eyes wide as they found the path through the unfamiliar chaos. Isabella had a piece of paper with Mrs Austin's address on it, and a little money remaining in her purse, so she used the last of her resolve to hire another cab to take them to Mrs Austin's residence in the city. She just had to hope that Mrs Austin would receive them, that her mother's old friend would not support Daniel in this moment.

The cab pulled up outside a narrow townhouse on a quiet road, and Isabella tipped the driver before steeling her courage again and walking to the front door. It was certainly too late for visitors, especially unannounced ones, and the maid looked confused when she saw the three unfamiliar girls at the door. At first, she seemed reluctant to allow them in at all, and then Mrs Austin appeared at the top of the stairway, dressed for sleep. She took one look at Isabella and hurried down the steps to meet her.

"Isabella," she said. "My goodness. What are you doing here? What has happened?"

"Mrs Austin," Isabella said. Words seemed to fail her. The image of Clare Swindon and her husband lying in bed flashed before her eyes again, and she fought back a sob.

"Oh, Isabella," Mrs Austin said. She hurried forward and placed a gentle hand on her shoulder. "Come inside, all of you. I am certain we can get to the bottom of whatever this is." Isabella, exhausted, finally safe, collapsed into sobs.

CHAPTER 9

*I*sabella lay in bed for days. She wanted to sleep, to find solace in the oblivion it offered, but her mind would not allow her to rest. So she simply kept the curtains drawn and stared at the walls of the chamber, refusing all entreaties for her to rise or eat. She had used all her strength holding herself and her dignity together as she fled with her sisters, and now that they were all safe and far away, she could not motivate herself even to sit up or speak. Mrs Austin heard some of the tale from a distraught Tabitha, and pieced together the rest herself. She was a widow herself, a city dweller and not at all naive, and she understood both what Tabitha was unwilling to say and what Tabitha herself may have missed. And although Mrs Austin was startled by the sudden appearance of three girls she did not know well, she felt responsible for Isabella's plight now. She had been the one to suggest the marriage. She had vouched for Daniel Kimble and insisted that he would treat her as well as she deserved. Now her friend's daughter was heartbroken and alone, without even that house in the slums to call her own. Yes, Mrs Austin would help her.

But as the days passed, Mrs Austin grew more and more

concerned. Isabella refused to rise or to eat. She stared blankly at the wall whenever anyone tried to speak to her, even her sisters, and could barely be coaxed to drink a single sip of water. After several days, she developed a fever, and her eyes took on a dazed expression as sweat beaded on her brow. Mrs Austin called in the doctor, but after a quick examination, he diagnosed exhaustion and heartbreak, and recommended rest, sunlight and company as the best possible cures.

So Mrs Austin pulled open the heavy drapes, letting sunlight spill onto Isabella's bed, and made sure that someone was always with her young friend, morning and night. Sometimes, the women would read to her, or chat to her about the sights of London, but Isabella rarely responded. She seemed utterly broken.

Isabella, for her part, was barely aware of what she was thinking. She only knew that she had failed. Daniel had found her inadequate, and this was her punishment for her failure. She had begged him to help raise her standards to fit into his world, and he had rebuffed her with a smile every time. He had lied to her, while betraying her in her own house. Isabella had trusted him, had even loved him, and it had led to this.

After a week, Isabella began to rouse from bed, but every bite of food she ate led her to vomit. The doctor was called again, and he examined Isabella with a grave expression on his face before stepping outside the room to speak to Mrs Austin.

"What is the matter with her?" Mrs Austin asked him. She spoke in a low voice, but Isabella could hear every word through the crack in the door. "Is she very ill?"

"Only in her mind, I believe," the doctor said, and Isabella pressed her cheek to the cool cotton pillow, letting the words wash over her.

"But she has been so unwell," Mrs Austin said. "She has barely eaten."

"She has allowed sadness to overwhelm her," the doctor said, "but it is my sincere professional opinion that she must endeavour to cheer herself from now on. She is with child, Mrs Austin."

As tired as Isabella was, it took a long moment for the meaning of the words to sink in. She was pregnant.

"A baby?" Mrs Austin said, in a surprised whisper.

"I dare not tell her myself as yet," the doctor replied. "I do not know what harm the news might cause her. As for her symptoms, she is suffering from common issues in early pregnancy. They should fade with time. And I believe that once she begins to heal in her heart, the physical symptoms will lessen too. And it will be all for the better if she does so soon. Such stress will not be good for the baby."

Isabella pressed a hand to her still flat stomach, tears spilling from her eyes. She felt, upon hearing those words that she had already failed, somehow, as a mother and a protector for this child. She had been so heartbroken that she had failed to notice the symptoms. But she knew now. She tried to imagine herself as a mother, without Daniel beside her. What would he do, she wondered, when he found out about the child? He could not find out, she decided. She would not go back. She would stay with Mrs Austin for as long as she was allowed, and then she would pose as a widow. She was afraid of what the future would bring, but for the first time since she saw Daniel in bed with Miss Swindon, she seemed to have a future, and even if she could not recover for her own sake or the sake of her sisters, her unborn child had committed no crime, and she knew she had to recover and protect it.

So it was with horror that Isabella found herself bleeding barely a week later. She let out a loud shriek, bringing both her sisters and Mrs Austin running, and then collapsed into a chair while their host called for the doctor for a third time.

The news was the worst sort. Isabella had been pregnant, the doctor said, but she had now lost the baby. He admonished

Isabella, telling her that too much despair was bad both for her own body and for any child she might carry, and that some fresh air and exercise would have made all the difference in her pregnancy. He did not explicitly say that the miscarriage was Isabella's fault, but Isabella read the blame between his words, and she helplessly fell into an even deeper despair. What did she have to fight for, after all, when her despair had already killed the child inside her?

Mrs Austin insisted that it was nonsense, that many women lost their babies early in the pregnancy, that it was God's way and God's will, but the doctor's unspoken condemnation fit much closer with Isabella's own feelings of self-loathing, and she accepted it as truth. As the weeks passed, she rose from her bed, and even stirred herself to attend social engagements with Mrs Austin and her sisters, but her heart was broken, and she spoke little. She spent most of her time staring off into the distance, and she was constantly pale and weak, barely strong enough even for a walk around the park.

Mrs Austin grew desperate. Nothing seemed able to pull Isabella out of her despair. The only answer, she thought, would be Daniel, and he was hundreds of miles away, his respectability in tatters in Mrs Austin's eyes. No, she would not inflict him or his family on poor Isabella any further. Relief would have to come from some other avenue.

"I wish I knew what to do for her," Mrs Austin said, as she and the two younger sisters took tea. Isabella had been downstairs with them for part of the morning, but she had soon withdrawn, complaining of a slight headache. Mrs Austin said the same thing almost every day now, but so far no plan, no book, no new form of company was enough to bring life back to Isabella's eyes. If she had undergone normal heartbreak, Mrs Austin might have thought to introduce her to new young men, perhaps brighten up her month by taking her to a ball, but Isabella had never been one for parties, and Mrs Austin sensed that this heartbreak ran far deeper than a husband's betrayal. Isabella was grieving for her father, and for her mother too. She was grieving for a lifetime of struggle and suffering, that one ray of hope now torn cruelly away. Mrs Austin had no plans to abandon the sisters to the streets, but her presence did little to soothe Isabella's certainty of her own failings, and her heartbreak over all she had lost.

One evening, several months after the sisters' arrival in London, Mrs Austin received an invitation to attend the opening of a new musical play by one of her husband's old friends. Mr Arnold Banker had left a career in trade to invest in a theatre, and he was far more involved in the creative elements and day-to-day problems than most investors in the arts tended to be. He was excited by this new production, and he thought Mrs Austin and her new wards might appreciate the outing. He, like many people in Mrs Austin's social circle, had heard a little of their plight, although the details were kept quiet. There had been the sudden loss of a husband, and an unborn child soon afterwards, or so the gossip said. The girls from Liverpool were in need of a treat, and Mrs Austin too, after carrying the eldest through her despair.

Isabella showed no enthusiasm for the trip, any more than she showed enthusiasm for anything those days. But as the opening overture played and the players began to sing, Isabella's eyes focussed on the scene, and she sat up straighter in her chair. She seemed enraptured by the scenes unfurling on stage. Mrs Austin spent half the play just watching her young charge's face, as colour and life slowly crept back into her eyes and her skin. Isabella smiled at the music, laughed at the jokes, and when the heroine thought she had tragically lost her love, Isabella's eyes filled with tears. Isabella did not notice Mrs Austin's attention. She was too enthralled by the production to be aware of anything else occurring around her. She had loved to put on plays as a small child, but she had never actually seen one. There had been neither the time nor the money since her father died. But this… this was like experiencing another life, another world, as closely as if it were her own, and the heroine's pain seemed to nestle alongside Isabella's own sadness. As the heroine cried out her heartbreak, Isabella felt as though something was resolving within her, and when the happy ending finally came, tears spilled down Isabella's cheeks as she soaked in the catharsis and wondered if, maybe, just maybe, she might one day be happy again too.

"Did you like it, my dear?" Mrs Austin asked her, as they waited for a carriage outside.

"Yes," Isabella said, her voice a little hoarse from lack of use. "Very much." The two younger girls chattered about the events of the play, but Isabella remained quiet until they returned to the house. Then Isabella withdrew to the music room, and the house rang with the tentative notes of the pianoforte. Isabella was recreating one of the tunes from the production, Mrs Austin realised, the song from when the heroine thought all hope had been lost. Isabella stumbled with the keys, pressing the wrong notes more often than right at first, but soon she had mastered it, and the delicate tune rang out as surely and strongly as if Isabella had composed the tune herself.

The next day, Isabella returned to the pianoforte, first playing familiar tunes, then experimenting with the notes herself. Mrs Austin had been loath to leave Isabella alone even for a moment these past months, in case Isabella saw fit to hurt herself, but as long as she could hear her notes on the pianoforte, she felt reassured that her charge was safe.

"I did not know she liked music so well," Mrs Austin said to Tabitha, as they took their lunch. Isabella had not left the piano room for a moment, not even to eat.

"Oh, yes," Tabitha said. "She was always making up songs and stories and plays when we were children, before apa died. She would invent little tunes in the house we shared with Mr

Kimble too. I thought perhaps she would never touch the instrument again, because Mr Kimble was the one who taught her the piano, although she plays much better than he does now, and he shouldn't be given any credit for her ability in my opinion."

"She likes to compose?" Mrs Austin asked.

Tabitha nodded. "Always fun, silly songs, the sort that make jest about people, but only in a way that you know she really loves them and means no sort of harm. And stories, of course. Izzy always loved stories."

Mrs Austin became lost in thought. She had always thought, even before this, that a woman needed a project to occupy her, whether that project was a husband or children or some great charitable pursuit. Stillness was not good for any soul, whether man or woman, and stillness was all that Isabella had experienced these past few months, after a lifetime of hectic activity. If she were to feel useful, she might come out of her deep melancholy. And if music gave the girl joy, then music she must have.

The theatre owner, Mr Banker, was always eager for new plays. He often espoused the need to get children into the theatre with their parents, so that they became lifelong attendees as they grew. But he had little to offer such an audience specifically, for he never had children himself, and did not appear to like them all that much. He was unlikely to consider it suitable for a young woman to write plays for a general audience, but if she were to pitch Isabella as a potential author of plays for children, complete with a few fun songs and a lot of jokes, Mr Banker must surely be willing to give her a chance.

Full of excitement for her new plan, Mrs Austin bustled off to grab some paper and a pen.

CHAPTER 10

When Daniel woke up on that fateful afternoon in his home in Liverpool, his first reaction was horror. His second reaction was rage. He had no memory of what had occurred that afternoon, but he knew, deep in his bones, that he would never do anything to hurt or betray Isabella if he could help it. As he awoke with Clare lying beside him, the evidence seemed clear. But Daniel had no love or affection for Miss Clare Swindon, and only temporary madness could have driven him to this situation, even without Isabella to consider. When he thought about his wife's feelings and reputation, he felt certain that some foul play was at work, because he would never betray her of his own free will.

He shouted at Clare to explain what she had done, and when she simply looked coyly at him, he ordered her out of the house at once. He dreaded Isabella and her sisters' return, unable to imagine how he would explain himself, until the hour grew late and he realised that her carpet bag and her few possessions were gone, along with her sisters'. She had not taken a single thing that she had not brought with her to the house, not a book or a hairpin, but Daniel felt, with certain despair, that she was gone.

He called on his mother in desperation, and she informed him that they had ended their outing late afternoon, and she had not heard from Isabella since. She looked surprised and concerned by Daniel's panic, but when he said his wife was missing, she merely shrugged and said that you could not expect a woman like that to stay around for long.

Daniel contacted the cafe where Isabella had worked and even wrote to Mrs Austin, on the slim hope that Isabella and her sisters had taken refuge with her in London, but the cafe owner knew nothing, and Mrs Austin did not reply. After a few weeks of silence, Daniel, feeling desperate now, resolved to travel down to London to pay Mrs Austin a visit. Surely she must know *something*. He was growing afraid that his wife had done something drastic and irreversible.

He had resolved to take the train down that weekend, and began to put plans into place, when he received a letter from his mother, asking for his attendance at her house as soon as he possibly could. Daniel did not dare to hope that she had news about Isabella, but he hurried there anyway, desperate for news. But when he stepped into the drawing room, he was greeted by a pale-faced Clare Swindon and her furious looking father.

Daniel's mother had raised him to uphold the highest values of politeness and propriety, but when he saw Clare, he saw red. He still had been unable to deduce precisely what had occurred that day, but he knew it had hurt Isabella deeply, and even though he must carry much of the blame, Clare had some scheming part in it, he knew.

"No," he said, fighting to keep his voice level. "I told you, Miss Swindon, that I did not wish to see you. If you thought you might meet with me today, you have been sorely mistaken."

"Sit down, young man," Clare's father, Mr Swindon, said, "or I will make you sit down." He was a broad-chested man with a well-groomed walrus moustache, and although Daniel did not do business with him often, he certainly knew of Mr Swindon's excellent reputation in trade and shipping. The man had always been jolly around Daniel before, but he looked furious now.

"Calm down, please, all of you," Daniel's mother said, carefully closing the drawing room door behind them. "Shouting will not solve any of this."

"Your son being more of a gentleman would have solved this!" Mr Swindon said, and Clare looked down, blushing rather delicately.

Daniel looked at each person in the room and shook his head. "What is happening here?" he asked. "What is going on?"

"What is happening," Mr Swindon shouted, "is that you have disrespected my only daughter and left her in a delicate condition, and now you are going to tell me what you are going to do about it."

"A delicate condition?" Daniel repeated. "That is impossible."

"It certainly is not impossible, from what my daughter has told me," Mr Swindon said. "Where is your wife, eh, boy? What made her leave so suddenly? Do not try to lie to me about what you have done, when the evidence is plainly against you."

Daniel shook his head, trying to clear the desperate buzzing that filled it, drowning out his thoughts. He needed to think. He did not remember anything that happened that afternoon, and Clare could not lie about this. He could feel his hands shaking as he took in what that meant. He had spent the past several weeks hoping that there had been some mistake, some trick to it, but clearly there had not.

"You are certain?" he said quietly to Clare.

She lifted her chin and met his gaze directly. "Completely certain, Mr Kimble," she said, her voice steady and full of dignity. "I would not mistake such a thing."

No, Daniel supposed that she would not. She would not have

informed her father unless she was quite sure there was no doubt or other choice.

"You will have to marry her," Mr Swindon said. "There is nothing else for it. I had hoped for a man with a little more respect, as my daughter's husband, but it is the only possible solution now."

"I cannot marry her," Daniel said. Yes, that fluttering feeling in his chest was definitely panic. "I am already married."

"And where is your wife?" Mr Swindon asked. "Gone, or so I hear. You will end that marriage and marry my daughter, to make amends for this grave insult against both her and me."

"I will not end my marriage," Daniel said. "Never!"

"Daniel, my dear." His mother put a comforting hand on his arm. "You already ended your marriage with your actions. I must admit I was horrified to hear the truth, when Clare and her father came to me. But what is done is done now. Isabella has left, and your future, and your reputation, lie here, with Clare and the baby."

"No," Daniel said. It was difficult to think clearly, but he was certain on this point, at least. "I will not leave Isabella. I am sorry, Clare, for whatever part I played in this. But I have no memory of anything occurring between us. I cannot abandon Isabella further. Surely one betrayal is enough."

"And what about your betrayal of Clare?" his mother asked. "Of me and your father and our family name? I will not have my grandchild born out of wedlock. You and Clare will marry, and that is final."

"I am sorry, Mother," Daniel said. "But I will not!" He felt pulled in two directions, without anything solid left for him to stand on. Everything he had ever learned, everything he had ever believed, told him that he must do the honourable thing and stick by Clare, if what she claimed was true. Everything inside him also told him that he would never dishonour Isabella or himself like that willingly, and that to force a divorce against

Isabella now would be an even greater betrayal. Isabella may have left him for good, but she still had the respectability of marriage around her. If she were to become divorced, she would be destroyed in the eyes of society for good.

Of course, if he did not divorce Isabella, then Clare would be destroyed in the eyes of society instead, and Clare's social circles were far closer to home. But he could not harm Isabella any further, not on purpose, not when he had other choices open to him.

"I am sorry," he said again. "I know you are disappointed. Please excuse me." He turned and began to walk for the door, and Mr Swindon strode after him.

"Wait one moment, boy!" he said. "You intend to leave my daughter like this?"

Daniel could not bear to say it aloud, so he simply stared back at the man. "There is nothing else I can do."

"If you ruin her for this," Mr Swindon said, "I will ruin you. Your name will be mud, boy. I will not have to inform them of the truth about my daughter. I will find other means to ruin you. Your career is done. Kimble Freighters is over. You will be the poor wastrel that you deserve to be."

Daniel bowed his head. "Then I am sorry for it, sir," he said. "It is certainly not what my father would have wished for. But no other choice remains for me. Good day to you."

And before anyone could say another word, Daniel strode from the room.

CHAPTER 11

The next that Daniel heard, Clare Swindon had moved in with his mother to receive real familial support and escape her father's wrath. Daniel truly was sorry for it. He had never particularly liked Clare, but he did not believe she deserved this.

With the situation as it was, he gave up on the idea of going to London in search of Isabella. His wife, wherever she was, was better off without his presence. Even if he could find her, he could never convince her to return now, with the truth of Clare awaiting her. It was cowardly, he knew, but he did not want to have to tell Isabella all that had occurred. He had clearly insulted her enough that day, insulted her so deeply that she had left without a single word. How would she react to this?

His mother sent him several more pleading letters, but Daniel ignored them. He was plagued by a constant headache, and he waited for Mr Swindon's retaliation, but for a few days, at least, it did not come. He guessed that his mother must have persuaded Mr Swindon to have a little patience, for all of their sakes. His mother could be very persuasive when she wanted to be, and if she wanted to believe that Daniel would change his mind, then she would believe it and convince everyone around her of the same thing too.

But Daniel knew, without hesitation, without doubt, that he could not change his mind. He would support Clare in all the ways he could, but he could not, would not, divorce Isabella to marry her.

So it was with some surprise that Daniel received a message from a barrister of his acquaintance, a Mr Barrington, requesting that Daniel call upon him at his office at his earliest convenience. The note made no mention of what matter might need to be discussed, but Mr Barrington worked with the registrar, and Daniel could only guess that his mother had reached out to him and told him something of the predicament. Not all of it, perhaps, not the truth about Clare, but enough to suggest that her son wished a speedy and subtle divorce.

Daniel was so furious at his mother's meddling that at first he resolved not to attend. But as his temper cooled, he decided that would be a mistake. He would not insult his acquaintance by ignoring the letter, for Mr Barrington could not know the true nature of the situation, and if Daniel attended the meeting, he would find out what she had been saying about her son and his intentions.

So Daniel made his way across Liverpool to Mr Barrington's office, and was surprised when the older man welcomed him in immediately. Mr Barrington was a tall, thin gentleman in his fifties, a dab hand at cards and a keen observer of the human species, and although Daniel had had little private conversation with the man, he respected him and was familiar enough with his ways to immediately understand how seriously he was taking this matter.

"Mr Kimble," Mr Barrington said. "Thank you for calling on me. I hope you are well." He did not wait for Daniel's reply before he continued. "I have something of a grave and delicate matter that I must discuss with you. I sincerely hope you do not believe I am interfering in your affairs when I tell you this, but I could not stand by and remain silent, when injustice such as this was afoot."

Daniel nodded. "If this is about Miss Swindon—"

"It is," Mr Barrington said, "but not in the way that you think. Please, be seated." He gestured at the free seat across from his desk, and Daniel sat down reluctantly. "A couple of days ago, your mother contacted my office, requesting a certificate of divorce. She informed me that you wished to avoid the public messiness and embarrassment for the woman in question, and so needed things handled as subtly as possible. Once this was complete, she informed me that you would need a new writ of marriage, this time to one Miss Clare Swindon."

Daniel jumped to his feet. "How dare she?" he asked. "I told her that I would not go along with her scheme."

"Yes, I quite understand, Mr Kimble," Mr Barrington said. "Please sit down and listen. I have not yet reached my point."

Daniel did as he was asked.

"I of course wished to help you and your family in any way I could," Mr Barrington continued, "but I found it somewhat odd that you did not make the request in person. You are quite the businessman, Mr Kimble. I did not believe you needed your mother to take care of your affairs. So I sent my son with a note to your mother's house, inquiring after more information, and he overheard the most shocking conversation as he approached. I trust, Mr Kimble, that Miss Swindon has informed you she is expecting a child?"

Daniel nodded. He did not know what else he could say.

"I am sorry to tell you, Mr Kimble, that she appears to be lying. My son overheard the entire thing. Your mother and Miss Swindon were discussing what they were to do when you found out the truth of Miss Swindon's condition, that she was in fact not expecting at all. I am appalled to say it, Mr Kimble, but as my son tells it, your mother informed Miss Swindon that she would simply drug you, as she did the last time, and this time Clare must do everything within her power to ensure a pregnancy occurred."

Daniel stared at him. He could not quite make Mr Barrington's words make sense. If he was understanding correctly, Mr Barrington was telling him that his mother admitted to drugging him on the day that Isabella left. She had drugged him and forced him into a compromising position, while— yes. She had invited Isabella and both her sisters out of the house to allow Clare to set up that shocking tableau, and then brought Isabella home at the appointed time to discover it.

It sounded preposterous, too farfetched to be real, but it was the first thing he had heard about this entire affair that made sense in his heart. He would not have betrayed Isabella, and he did not recall doing so. But Isabella had warned him that his mother disliked her, had she not? She had been concerned about Clare. Yet Daniel had underestimated them both as enemies, reassuring Isabella that there was nothing to fear. And now Isabella was gone, and Daniel was trapped in this web.

He stood up abruptly. "I— thank you, Mr Barrington. I greatly appreciate this favour you have done me. If you will excuse me, I believe I need to speak with my mother."

"I would not advise it," Mr Barrington said.

Daniel turned back to face him. "You would not advise it?" he repeated. "These women have drugged me, lied to me, and tried to trick me into a life of disgrace. What sort of man would I be if I did not go and confront them this very instant?"

"A wise one," Mr Barrington said, "which I know you to be, Mr Kimble. This is only hearsay, you understand. It is not *proof*. Certainly, your mother came to me against your wishes, but that is easily excusable, is it not, as the actions of a mother wishing to protect a young lady and her future grandchild? Anything else is far-fetched indeed."

"But you clearly believe it," Daniel said, "or you would not have informed me."

"I do," Mr Barrington said. "My son is a trustworthy source, not prone to gossip, and he seemed truly shocked by what he had overheard. And if I had any doubt, your belief in the story would have dispelled it. Still, it will not be enough to convince others. Your mother will deny it, and why not? The story sounds quite mad. You will need to gather more proof if you wish to force them to admit to their crimes."

"Then what am I to do?" Daniel asked.

"Stay alert," Mr Barrington said. "Be certain that they cannot trap you into doing something you do not wish to do. It seems to me that, given enough time, your mother and Miss Swindon will be forced to act again or admit to their lies when no child appears. So you must be alert to any and all tricks, and stand firm against them. They were already careless enough to give the game away once. Surely they will misstep again."

Daniel did not like the plan at all. He wanted to run to his mother's house and confront her over what she had done. He wanted to bring this horrific chapter of his life to an end, so that he could search for Isabella with all the proof he needed to convince her to return. But as he thought about it, he realised his error. Isabella had chosen to leave, and he could not cause her further pain by begging her to return, even if he discovered where she lived. She was too good for him and his family. He would not bring her back here, to potentially be subject to his mother's harmful meddling. If his mother was willing to drug her own son to end his marriage to Isabella and force the marriage with Clare, what would she be willing to do to a girl she had made clear she had no affection or regard for whatsoever? It would be neither safe nor just to bring Isabella and her sisters back while his mother might still scheme.

Mr Barrington was right. First, Daniel needed proof. And for that, as much as he loathed to admit it, he would need to be patient.

CHAPTER 12

Mrs Austin's plan for Isabella turned out to be nothing less than a stroke of brilliance. Although Isabella initially demurred, claiming that her songs were just her own little fancies and she could never aspire to become a professional, Mrs Austin convinced her to write a short children's musical for Mr Banker, and he was so delighted with it that he immediately commissioned two more. Over several months, she wrote multiple plays, splitting her earnings between saving and paying Mrs Austin for her and her sisters' keep. Little by little, writing and music pulled Isabella out of her despair. Although she still got lost in thought sometimes, and was always a little more melancholy than she had been before, Isabella rediscovered her passion for life and her hope for the future, and Mrs Austin and Isabella's sisters delighted to see her smiling again.

This was not to say that her new career was always easy. Every successful play added more pressure for her to write an even bigger success, and far more potential disappointment if she did not succeed. The other writers associated with the theatre were often cold with Isabella, and Isabella rather got the sense that this class of artists and university graduates saw her as an intruder and an upstart, a cafe girl from the North daring to assume she might step into their world. The fact that she was a woman did not help either. More and more she yearned to work on something bigger than these short children's plays, but she was a woman, and if she was threatening as a children's playwright, she would have been utterly unacceptable as a writer for adults.

But, Isabella thought, she was lucky to have Mrs Austin's friend, Mr Banker, to support her. He praised her plays and always commissioned more, no matter what some of his other writers thought, and he took Isabella under his metaphorical wing, teaching her the official language of the stage and suggesting plays that might delight her. Isabella often found herself having dinner with her sisters, Mrs Austin, Mr Banker and his wife, and she felt cosy and safe in this new social circle she had built. Mr Banker's wife, a friendly if slightly dull woman in her forties, insisted that Isabella call her Matilda, like they were old friends, and then even Mr Banker started to call her Isabella and requested that the girls all call him Arnold. That last part felt a little strange to Isabella, but Daniel had more than proved that she did not fully understand the rules of propriety or the whims of the rich, and as Arnold was a married man and she was a married woman, and Arnold's wife did not seem to mind, Isabella put the worry aside.

One evening, about ten months after the sisters' arrival in London, Isabella was working late at the theatre. Although Isabella could write on the pianoforte in Mrs Austin's study, she did not like to do so too often, in case she disturbed the rest of the house. Everyone always insisted that they did not mind, but Isabella did not believe that anyone could hear her playing the same few notes with slight variations over and over for an hour without their temper being at least slightly rattled. Besides, Isabella liked the quiet, and if no plays were being performed, the theatre offered plenty of that. She liked the way the music rang inside the old walls, and felt like memories of songs and stories from before lingered there, ready to inspire her.

She was so absorbed in her work that she did not hear Arnold enter. When she reached the end of her composition, he applauded, and she jumped, her knees knocking against the pianoforte.

"Mr Banker," she said. "I mean, Arnold. I did not see you there."

"Hard at work, I see," Arnold said. He moved closer, reaching over her shoulder to pick up the sheet music she had been working on. "A piece for the latest play?"

"Yes," Isabella said. She took in a deep breath, forcing herself to relax. She felt tense, for some reason, with Arnold so close behind her, but he was her friend and her mentor, and they had been alone in the theatre together many times before. "What did you think of it?"

"Delightful," he said. "As always." He placed the music back on its stand and slid his hand down to rest on Isabella's shoulder. "You are a star, Isabella. I cannot thank Mrs Austin enough for introducing you to me. You will be my secret weapon, you'll see."

"Thank you," Isabella said quietly. She moved to stand, and Arnold's hand dropped from her shoulder. "I've been working hard on it."

"You always do." Arnold clapped his hands together as she stepped away. "Isabella, my dear, I've been thinking. You are so very talented. I think you might be ready to move on from this children's writing. Create something for a wider audience, hm?"

Isabella beamed. "Do you really think so?"

"Yes, certainly, my dear, I do." Arnold reached out and took her hands in his, and Isabella squeezed his hands back, feeling lighter than air. "You are deliciously talented. But," he continued, and Isabella felt her stomach drop slightly, "we must discuss the issue of exclusivity, of course."

"Exclusivity?" Isabella tried to gently pull her hands away, but Arnold's grip was firm.

"I cannot foster a protégé as talented as you and risk you running off and taking all my investment with you to another theatre or another man, now, can I? And it will be such a risk to put my faith in a young woman such as yourself. A woman, a playwright? I believe in you, my dear, but others may not, and the risk to me will be great indeed. I need some assurances."

"What sort of assurances?" Isabella asked, fearing what the answer might be.

"Be my mistress, Isabella," he said, tightening his grip on her hands and tugging her closer still. "You are a beautiful young woman. You should not be forced to live as a widow forever. And I like you very much indeed."

"Arnold, no," Isabella said. She wrenched her hands away. "You are married!"

"Which is why I could not marry you," Arnold said. "I would not hurt Matilda like that, even if you were unwed yourself."

"But you will hurt Matilda by asking me to be your mistress?" Isabella asked. She was shocked. A woman had ruined her life by dallying with her husband. She would not inflict that same pain on anyone else, and Matilda was a *friend*. Arnold – Mr Banker –

was also supposed to be a friend, although she was rapidly regretting that assumption now.

"Come now, Isabella," Mr Banker said, reaching for her again. She darted back, out of reach. "You must have expected this. I cannot hire you and support you for nothing."

"You hire me and support me because of my talent," Isabella said. "Because my plays bring in audiences."

"I could bring in audiences with a far less controversial playwright than you, my dear," he said, and his tone had turned steely now. "Are you not grateful for all I have done to support you?"

"I am," Isabella said firmly. "However, I worked hard for it. I deserved the success I got. One man already nearly destroyed my life, sir, after I made an agreement with him for my own well-being. I refuse to risk that happening again. I am sorry, but I must decline your offer." She tilted her chin up, meeting Mr Banker's gaze with all the pride and defiance she could muster. Mr Banker's face turned red with anger.

"If you reject me," he said, "you reject all the support I have given you. How dare you be so ungrateful!"

"How dare you proposition me like this," Isabella retorted. "Both my good sense and my honour insist that I reject you, sir. I will not be beholden to you, not for anything!"

"I will ruin you," he said, in a low, dangerous voice. "Reject me now, and I will make sure you come back to me, begging on your knees."

"That will never happen," Isabella said. "I will never disgrace myself before you."

"Get out!" Mr Banker spat. "Get out of this theatre and do not even think of coming back until you are ready to grovel."

She hesitated. "You still owe me for the latest play."

"I owe you *nothing*, Miss Thorne. Leave now, before I call the police."

Isabella stared back at him for a long moment. He was shaking with fury, but then, so was she. She had believed him to be a true, honest friend, a reliable acquaintance of Mrs Austin and a genuine believer in Isabella's talents. How wrong she had been. But how dare he speak to her so? How dare he threaten her livelihood and her honour in this way?

She did not need him, she decided. He was just another burden life had thrown her way, and she did not need him to succeed. She stared at him for a long moment, and then she picked up her skirts and swept away without looking back.

CHAPTER 13

Isabella was so filled with indignation and anger that she took the long way home to Mrs Austin's townhouse, her feet hammering out a fierce rhythm on the cobbles of the street. *How dare he?* She thought, over and over again. *How* dare *he?* Then she thought of telling Mrs Austin about what had happened, and she felt even greater anger and dread. Mrs Austin had supported Isabella so completely over the past months. She had helped keep Isabella alive when Isabella herself had given up on the cause. How could Isabella now tell her that one of her oldest friends was a cad and a crook? Would Mrs Austin even believe Isabella when she told her?

She would, Isabella decided at once. Of course she would. Mrs Austin was the sisters' greatest ally and friend, and she despised misconduct. She had forsaken her acquaintance with Daniel and his mother, had she not, after Isabella told her what happened? Still, Isabella found herself walking a little slower at the idea of having to tell Mrs Austin what had happened, and a good two hours had passed since the confrontation by the time she reached Mrs Austin's door.

Isabella felt somewhat calmer now, and her hands were steady as she entered the house.

"Isabella?" Mrs Austin asked. Her voice came from the sitting room.

"Yes, Mrs Austin," Isabella said. "I am sorry I am back so late."

"Come here, please," Mrs Austin said. "I need to speak with you."

It seemed impossible that Mrs Austin already knew what had happened, but her tone was grave. Had she guessed Mr Banker's intentions before? Did she intend to warn Isabella now? Or was she simply angry that Isabella had returned home later than she expected?

Isabella entered the sitting room to find Mrs Austin in a chair by the fire, her face tense with anger.

"I'm here, Mrs Austin," she said tentatively. "What has happened?"

"You just missed Mr Banker," Mrs Austin said carefully. "He departed not half an hour ago."

Isabella's stomach dropped. He must have rushed here by carriage as soon as Isabella left the theatre, to have arrived and departed before Isabella came home. "What did he want?" she asked softly.

"He came with information regarding you," Mrs Austin said, "and your conduct. He is most concerned. I must admit myself thoroughly deceived. I thought you a good and virtuous girl, Isabella, injured by circumstance. But Mr Banker has informed me of your affairs."

"Affairs?" Isabella repeated, horror struck.

"With drinkers and gamblers and all kinds of lowlifes, not to mention with other playwrights at the theatre. Mr Banker's establishment is a place of the arts, Isabella, not a brothel! You disgrace yourself, and you disgrace me by your association."

"Mr Banker is lying!" Isabella shouted. "I would never do such a thing." She could feel her cheeks burn, half from embarrassment over the accusations and half from her fury at their injustice.

"What cause would he have to lie?" Mrs Austin asked. "He told me you were with one of your lovers tonight, and he came here out of concern for you, and for your sisters!"

"He did no such thing," Isabella said. "He is lying to ruin my reputation. He propositioned me tonight, when we were alone at the theatre. I refused, and he told me he would ruin me for it. That is why he is lying!"

"I wish I could believe you, Isabella," Mrs Austin said, "but I am afraid I am no fool, to be taken advantage of twice. Mr Banker is a married man, and he is devoted to his wife."

"Not devoted enough," Isabella said. "I swear to you, he asked me to be his mistress. He told me he would make me suffer if I refused him."

Mrs Austin considered Isabella for a long moment, and Isabella had the wild hope that Mrs Austin might believe her. Alas, Mrs Austin shook her head, her lips pressed together in disappointment. "I have given you so much, Isabella, and you repay me in this way. With lies and deceit and immoral behaviour of the sort that I can hardly bear to think on. You bring disgrace to yourself and your sisters, and by association, you bring disgrace to me as well. What must people think of me, when they learn of your dallying? What would they have continued to think, if Mr Banker had not informed me of the truth?"

"He is lying!" Isabella said again. Tears burned in her eyes. "Please believe me, Mrs Austin. I'm grateful for everything you've done for me, and you know me. You must."

But Mrs Austin was shaking her head. "Mr Banker has been a lifelong friend to me," she said. "And I should not be surprised. You grew up under rough, difficult circumstances. It is not surprising that you have picked up some of the habits of the slums. But I cannot allow them to exist here."

"Habits of the slums?" Isabella repeated. She felt as though Mrs Austin had slapped her. "How dare you—"

"I am not a heartless woman," Mrs Austin said, cutting Isabella off. "I will not throw you and your sisters out on the street tonight. But you must depart tomorrow. Find somewhere to rent, or go to the workhouse if you must. Or return to your husband, if you have the fare for the train. But I will not have you in my house if this is your behaviour."

"Mrs Austin," Isabella said, her heart breaking. "Please."

Mrs Austin turned away to look again at the fire. "I suggest you go and pack," she said. "You must depart first thing tomorrow."

Tears running down her face, Isabella turned away and headed upstairs to tell her sisters the news.

CHAPTER 14

Tabitha and Abigail were furious with Mrs Austin and Mr Banker on Isabella's behalf, but nothing they could say would sway a heart set so firmly against them. The girls departed the following morning with the few possessions they had arrived with, and Mrs Austin did not appear to wish them goodbye.

The sisters were lucky that Isabella had always been prudent with her writing income. Although she had paid Mrs Austin for their room and board, she had saved almost all of the rest, and it was enough to rent a small cottage on the outskirts of the city. The place was run-down and afflicted with dampness, but the fireplace still warmed it well enough, and it had three separate rooms, which still struck the girls as luxury after a life growing up in the Liverpool slums.

But rent on the cottage would be due weekly, and Isabella's savings would not last forever. If the girls were to survive, they would have to work. Isabella had considered the workhouse for a brief second the night Mrs Austin turned them away, but that was no solution except in the direst of circumstances. They would be mistreated terribly, unable to earn any real money, and forced to stay in the dorms of the workhouse where she knew suffering and abuse were rife. She would do anything she could to keep herself and her sisters away from that place. Instead, she went around town, enquiring in cafes if they had any need for additional help. Tabitha and Abigail both found work easily enough, but Isabella, as a married woman, was turned away, and she began to feel desperate to be useful. Perhaps she could find work doing laundry or mending, she thought, as their mother had done.

The younger sisters came home from work so exhausted that they collapsed directly into bed, but Isabella stayed up late, writing out plans in the light of the last embers of the fire. She would not be defeated by Mr Banker's villainy. There had to be something she could do.

It was lucky, in the end, that Isabella was so desperate. If she had not been so eager to find solutions, late into the night, she may not have fallen asleep in her chair in the living room, within earshot of the front door. She may not have heard footsteps around the house, or the faint crackle of flame that followed them. As it was, Isabella awoke slowly, blinking sleepily as she became aware of an acrid smell in the air.

The entire front wall of the cottage, including the front door, was aflame, and the air was thick with smoke. She jumped to her feet as she became aware of it, and then broke down into a fit of coughing.

"Tabitha!" she gasped. "Abigail!" She stumbled across the smoke-filled room to the bedroom where her sister's slept. Tabitha was already sitting up, looking dazed, but Abigail was fast asleep.

"Out the window," Isabella said to Tabitha. "Quick." She shook her youngest sister awake, and began dragging her by the arm before she was fully conscious.

"Isabella?" Abigail murmured. "What's happening?"

"Fire," Isabella said, as calmly and no-nonsense as she could. "Come on."

The smoke was billowing thick now, and Isabella could hear the creaks and moans of the cottage as the flames consumed its front walls. Isabella pushed Abigail out of the window and then scrambled after her, and the three sisters ran as fast as they could to the road. Tabitha and Abigail were both dressed in their nightgowns, the white cloth black from the smoke, their hair loose around their shoulders. Only Isabella was dressed, and her hair was half-collapsed too from her nap by the hearth.

"What do we do?" Abigail asked.

Isabella shook her head. They could not call the fire brigade. The house was not insured, and no one would come and extinguish the flames for free. "The police," she said, after a long moment staring at the fire. "The police would help us."

But the constable, when he arrived, did not seem particularly interested in helping them at all. Isabella told him about Mr Banker's vow to ruin her, and the footsteps she had heard around the house just before the fire began, but the constable seemed more concerned with interrogating Isabella about her own actions. "Fell asleep in the front room, did you?" he asked her, with a knowing look in his eye. "Probably left a candle burning. It must've caught the drapes."

"It did not," Isabella said, even though she had left a candle burning, and anyone who investigated the husk of the burned-out cottage would find the metal candlestick holder she had left. "I tell you, someone came to the house and was sneaking around."

"There is no proof of that, miss," the constable said. "We can't go accusing good men of arson on the basis of one young woman's word, especially when there are far more likely explanations about."

"But please—" Isabella said. If the police concluded that the fire had been started by a forgotten candle, the landlord would blame her for what had happened too. She could not imagine a scenario in which the landlord would willingly forgive her without some sort of monetary compensation, and she had so little left in her savings. Would she be arrested for it? Would the landlord have her sent to debtors] prison for her inability to pay him for the property that had burned?

With nowhere else to go, the girls sat by the roadside while the house still smouldered until the landlord could be informed and chose to appear. They must have looked frightful, Isabella thought. Soot covered young girls in their nightclothes, sitting by the side of the road as the morning stretched on and people passed by on their business. Everyone seemed to glance at them, and some people narrowed their eyes or shifted their path to avoid them, like they were vagrants and their misfortune might be contagious if anyone got too close.

Isabella struggled not to sob. In a few short days, everything she had built for herself had been ripped from her again. Perhaps, she thought, she should have accepted Mr Banker's offer. At least then her sisters would still have money and a home and friends to support them. Tabitha and Abigail's future prospects had been ruined by the loss of Mrs Austin, far more than Isabella's had been. But no, she told herself, clenching her fists with resolve. She would not be under any man's thumb, no matter the cost. She would fight for her sisters and for herself, but she would never debase herself on a cruel man's whim. She would get justice somehow.

The landlord, when he arrived, was a short, rat-faced man; he took one look at the remnants of the cottage and began to scream at Isabella, spittle flying from his lips. Isabella tried to remain calm in response, but the landlord would not accept any excuse or apology, and Isabella found herself forced to offer the remains of her savings in recompense to escape him calling the police again and trying to have the sisters arrested. As flimsy as his claim was, Isabella's previous encounter with the constable suggested to her that the force would be far more likely to side with the landlord than with a girl like her.

"Well, there's nothing for it," Isabella said, in a bracing tone, as the girls stumbled away from their home and the last of their money. "We shall have to go to the workhouse, and start again."

"Surely there must be something else we could do," Abigail said, but Isabella sadly shook her head.

"We can't afford a place to live, Abby. It's go there or sleep on the streets, and we have a better chance of surviving this in there than out here." Isabella felt that familiar despair pressing down on her again, the hopelessness that had so overwhelmed her just a few months before. But she could not let it defeat her again, for her sisters' sakes. They had no more friends whose kindness they might rely upon. If they were to ever get out of the workhouse again, Isabella would have to be the one to do it.

She would not allow men like Daniel and Mr Banker to defeat them.

CHAPTER 15

If Isabella had not already felt humiliated by circumstances, the girls' arrival at the workhouse would have changed that. As it was, Isabella faced down the rough treatment at the hands of the supervisors with resignation. A woman forced all three girls to strip, before scrubbing them down hard with soap and water to remove any vermin that might linger on their skin. They were then given drab grey uniforms to wear and sent off to start work at once. They were lucky, other workers at the workhouse told them later, that they were not separated, but as the sisters were all close enough in age and there was enough space in one dormitory for them all, the girls continued to sleep near one another and work the same shift together, weaving together pieces of rope with soon-calloused hands.

Isabella went to bed each night too exhausted to worry or cry, and she was grateful for it. She could not help feeling that she had failed her sisters, but she could not allow herself to fall into despair when they needed her now more than ever.

The one bright spot in their days now was Sunday afternoon, when they were allowed the luxury of a couple of hours of free time. The sisters would walk to a nearby park and spend the hours there, rain or shine, breathing in the fresh air and looking up at the open sky. On these days, Isabella would gather what scraps of paper she could get and write, while her sisters chatted and played. Isabella had lost all of her work along with all their other possessions in the fire, and she could not imagine anyone wishing to see the play written by a girl in the workhouse, but she needed to continue working and continue creating, or she would go mad. But for once, Isabella did not write about wild fantasies or fun moral tales for children. Her heart was broken once again, and she could not think how to mend it other than to write her way through it. Piece by piece, she turned the tragedy of her life into scenes and songs, and although it did not heal the hurt she had endured, it at least made her feel productive.

It was on one such Sunday, several months after the fire and the destruction of the cottage that Abigail found a recent newspaper abandoned atop a bench. Abigail missed the ability to access books almost more than she missed having a truly warm home and decent food, and she quickly snatched it up and brought it over to the other girls. They sat on the grass together in the sunshine and divided up the paper, each taking part and ravenously devouring the news and stories it offered.

"Look here, Izzy," Tabitha said, once she had read almost every word of the paper and had been driven to reading the advertisements in her desperation for entertainment. "There's a theatre here looking for a script writer. You could do that!"

"I don't know," Isabella said. "They're probably only willing to hire a man." Memories of Mr Banker's advances still haunted her, and she could no longer imagine any other theatre owner treating her with any more respect.

"Maybe not," Tabitha said. "Look." She jabbed the paper with her finger as she held it in front of her sister. "The advertisement was placed by a Madam Francine Majors. A *woman*. If a woman is running a theatre, surely she'll be willing to have other women working for her too."

"Perhaps," Isabella said warily, "but it isn't always so easy." She had seen enough of the world of theatre to know that women were a rare presence, and that those who did work in the industry were often as cruel if not crueller to aspiring women than the men, as though an increased female presence would threaten their own place.

"It's worth a try, though, isn't it?" Abigail asked. "You're so talented, Isabella. This could be your chance."

Isabella had thought that her work with Mr Banker had been her chance, and after the past few weeks in the workhouse and her humiliation of being evicted by Mrs Austin, she was beginning to doubt that she had ever had any talent at all. Perhaps Mr Banker had never admired her work, even from the beginning. Maybe he had only ever thought of her as a potential mistress, and not a creative mind to be supported.

But still, she tore the advertisement out of the paper, promising her sisters that she would consider it, and when she lay in her narrow bed that night, trying to find a comfortable position on the lumpy mattress, she could not stop thinking about it. Was she going to allow another cruel, selfish man to destroy her life and her belief in herself? Did all the joy of composing and the success she had seen vanish because one man had seen fit to take advantage of her?

Isabella could not give up yet, not when a chance had practically fallen into her lap.

But how could she leave the workhouse to answer the advertisement, when she was expected to work all day long?

In the end, Isabella took a risk and pretended to be unwell. The supervisor was not particularly sympathetic, but Isabella insisted that she was afraid she would vomit in the factory if she tried to work, and eventually her begging was enough to convince the supervisor to give her the afternoon off and send her out of the main building of the workhouse and across to the infirmary. Isabella walked dutifully towards the infirmary door until she was certain no one was watching her, and then she darted away, out onto the street.

The theatre on the advertisement was several miles away, and Isabella did not have any money for a cab, so she walked as fast as she dared in her workhouse uniform, moving briskly without drawing attention from anyone who might think she was running away.

The theatre, when she reached it, was small – smaller than Mr Banker's – with a few forlorn looking posters for plays attached to the front. Isabella went around the side to try and find the stage door, and then knocked timidly. When no one answered, she forced herself to knock again, harder, praying that this Madam Francine Majors was in.

Eventually, the door jerked open, and a short, plump woman dressed all in black peered out. She had half-moon spectacles on her nose and an irritated expression on her face as she peered at Isabella.

"Yes?" she said bluntly. "What?"

Isabella could feel herself blushing. "Madam Francine Majors?" she asked.

The woman jerked her head in agreement. "What of it?"

"I've come to answer your advertisement in the paper," Isabella said. She held up the clipping helpfully. "For a script writer?"

The woman looked Isabella up and down, her eyes narrowed. "You look like you've come from the workhouse," she said. "And you're young, too. Youth always thinks it has more talent than it does. Especially when it's desperate."

"I—" Isabella could not think how to argue with that. "I have written plays before," she said. "For children. For Mr Arnold Banker."

The woman snorted and spat on the ground. "Psh. Mr

Banker! He's a crook if I've ever seen one. Though I s'pose he doesn't put on any old rubbish at his theatre, either. But I'm not interested in children's plays."

"Maybe— maybe I could come in," Isabella said hopefully. "So we can talk."

The woman looked Isabella up and down again, and then nodded. "Fine," she said. "Haven't heard from anyone else about the advertisement, anyway. You can call me Madam Francine," she added over her shoulder, as she led the way back inside. "Everyone here does."

"Thank you," Isabella said. The space inside was dark, with only one small grimy window. Madam Francine seemed to have been working at a narrow desk. Papers and bills were piled high upon it, along with an oil lamp, and the entire rest of the space was crammed with costumes and props. They filled shelves and were piled on the floor, spilling out of chests and perched on extra chairs by the door.

"This is my theatre," Madam Francine said, "as I'm sure you've guessed, girl. Well, my last scriptwriter quit on me. He wanted more pay, but how could I pay him any more than I was? His plays were terrible. No one came to see them. We haven't put on a decent show in months, we're practically going out of business, and he asks for a raise? No. But now, I can't even put on *bad* plays, with him gone. It's better, in a way. I don't lose money paying the actors. But I don't make money either!"

"What sort of plays are you looking for?" Isabella asked. "I write musical plays, myself."

"Forgive my skepticism," Madam Francine said, "but as I said, you look young and desperate for money. That's not promising, from my perspective."

"I have experience," Isabella said. "And— here." She pulled out the script she had been working on, cobbled together on many different scraps of paper on several Sunday afternoons.

"This is what I've been writing recently. I haven't had access to a pianoforte, so I haven't been able to try out the tunes properly, but—"

"Is this supposed to convince me?" Madam Francine asked, looking skeptical. "It's all scraps and rags." But Madam Francine must have been desperate too, because she took the pages from Isabella and sat down at her desk, adjusting the glasses on her nose as she went.

She read for several minutes, and Isabella waited in silence, desperately trying to read her expression. Then Madam Francine gave an approving sort of grunt. "Not bad," she said. "You've got some talent, girl." She continued reading, nodding along as she went. After another few minutes, she grabbed a pen from the desk, and began to make notes alongside Isabella's words. "This is good," she said. "Really good." She looked back at Isabella. "How long did this take you?"

"A few Sundays," Isabella said.

"Hmm." She continued to scan the pages. "It'll need some work," she said. "But this is just the sort of story people are wanting to see. Its got tragedy and its got heart, and if you can make the audience cry and then feel better about it, you've got yourself a hit, in my experience." She considered Isabella for a moment. "You couldn't stay at the workhouse," she said firmly. "This'll take a lot of work. I can't have you working and sleeping somewhere else and barely able to spare a few hours here and there."

"I don't have anywhere else to live," Isabella said. "My home burned down, and

I—"

The woman waved her hand dismissively. "Sleep above the theatre," she said. "There's room for one there, if you don't mind being cramped, and you don't mind sharing with a couple of spiders. Here's what I'm thinking," Madam Francine said. "You just might be my ticket out of this mess that so-called writer left me in. So you live here, and we put on this play. We work on it, fix it up, *and* you star in it. You've got the look of a tragic damsel about you, far more than my other girls. I can't pay you while we're working on it, because I have barely any coin left, but you'll get room and board for your efforts, and I'll split the proceeds with you when it's done. Twenty percent will be yours. Can't say fairer than that, can I?"

If the play failed, Isabella thought, she would earn nothing from it. But then again, she already had nothing, and was already working for scraps. At least if she accepted this deal, she would be working on her dream again, and there was a chance, slim as it might be, that she would succeed.

"I have two younger sisters," Isabella said. "They're at the workhouse too. I'd want them to stay with me."

"There's barely room for one to sleep up there," Madam Francine said, "let alone three, but if you can manage it, by all means do so. If your sisters are willing to do some errands around here for me, I'll even feed them too."

"Oh, thank you!" Isabella said. She wanted to sing with relief. But she did not want to look unprofessional, or make Madam Francine regret her decision, so instead, she simply smiled. "I will make it all worth it for you," she said. "I promise."

CHAPTER 16

After Daniel discovered the truth about Clare and his mother, he withdrew from their society, so angry that he could hardly bear to see their faces or speak to them. He did not have any evidence of their behaviour, so he could not confront them, and he found himself growing increasingly morose, feeling trapped in his family and his job and all the expectations they presented him with.

He wrote to Mrs Austin twice, begging for any news about Isabella, but he did not receive a reply. His wife was long gone, his mother had betrayed him, and his life began to feel increasingly hollow, like all the things that should matter have been torn away.

In the end, he reached out to his mother's older brother, Uncle Kelvin, a somewhat sickly old man who Daniel did not know as well as he would like to. Uncle Kelvin had lived alone in London ever since his wife had died a couple of years before, and although his letters suggested he had something of a lively social life, always going to plays and museums, Daniel always got the feeling that he was rather lonely. Really, he told himself, he would be doing Uncle Kelvin a favour, offering the easiest and best sort of charity, if he travelled to stay with the old man and kept him company for a little while. Daniel did not want to admit that he needed the company as much as Uncle Kelvin might, but his feelings must have seeped through into his letter unintentionally, because Uncle Kelvin wrote back at once, insisting that Daniel travel down to London and stay for as long as he desired. *Real society is in London,* he wrote, in a scratchy, unstable hand. *It will do you good here, after that depressing Northern air.*

Daniel was relieved to arrive in the capital, and even more relieved when he discovered that his uncle was excellent company. Uncle Kelvin was quick witted and more well-read than Daniel thought he could ever hope to be, and every conversation was filled with clever jokes and intriguing allusions. Uncle Kelvin insisted on Daniel accompanying him to all of the best clubs, to the newly opened museums, to gatherings with popular new artists and the premieres of exciting new plays and shows. Although Daniel still missed Isabella terribly, and felt tremendous guilt for his part in what had happened, for the first time in a year he felt like himself again too, like the world had more to offer than his disappointment with himself.

"I managed to acquire us tickets for that new play at that little theatre on Liverpool Street," Uncle Kelvin said from his armchair one day, when Daniel emerged from his rooms. "The Times raved about it, as did the Spectator. It's been quite tricky to get my hands on tickets, let me tell you, but I've got a few tricks up the old sleeve yet."

"What is this one about?" Daniel asked idly, picking up the morning paper from the sideboard and seating himself in a chair beside his uncle.

"Oh, the usual sort of thing," Uncle Kelvin said. "Tragic orphan struggles to survive against the cruelties of the modern world and falls in love for her trouble. But the critics all say it's terribly moving, and I find myself in the mood for some song and tragedy."

"Excellent," Daniel said, still not fully listening. "I look forward to it."

So that evening, Daniel and Uncle Kelvin put on their semi-best jackets and took a cab to central London, where they visited the Brockhurst Theatre. Crowds had gathered in front of the doors, everyone talking excitedly about the most popular new show in town.

"Need a ticket, guv'ner?" a man asked, as Daniel and Uncle Kelvin approached. "I've got two just for you, special deal, if you're buying."

"We're not," Uncle Kelvin said, tapping the side of his nose in a conspiratorial manner. "We're all set, thank you."

The theatre was surprisingly small and dark inside, the seats cramped together, but Uncle Kelvin seemed delighted with the rustic nature of it all. He and Daniel settled into the seats and waited eagerly for the play to begin.

Or at least, Uncle Kelvin waited eagerly. Daniel found he was developing a slight headache from the noise of the people around him, and he rather wished that he could return home to Uncle Kelvin's house and spend some time alone. He almost considered pleading out to his Uncle and heading out to find a cab to take him back, when the orchestra began to play the overture, and the few lights around the audience dimmed. Daniel turned his attention back to the stage, determined to make the best of the evening, and then almost gasped out loud when the actress walked onto the stage.

It was Isabella.

It seemed so impossible that for a moment he thought he must be imagining things. Maybe he was more unwell than he had thought. But underneath the thick stage makeup and carefully styled hair, he recognised his Isabella's delicate features and the sound of her voice. When she broke into song, the theatre rang with the same sound he had heard so many times before, shy but beautiful, as she sang and wrote songs in the library of their house.

Daniel felt tears forming in his eyes as he watched his beloved singing her heart out. He knew now why so many people adored this play. Isabella was telling the story of her life, and every line of dialogue and note of song rang with real, deep emotion. She was utterly entrancing. Had Isabella collaborated with the playwright to create this? Or had she written it herself? Had her singing by the pianoforte led her here?

When the play drew to a close, Daniel leapt to his feet and gave a passionate standing ovation. Inspired by his enthusiasm, the rest of the audience followed suit, and Daniel's heart swelled to see the way that Isabella smiled at the crowd's approbation.

She was so close, he thought. He could walk up and talk to her. Ask her how she was. But as he saw her curtsey to the audience, joy shining from her face, Daniel knew that he could not allow himself to hurt her again. She had found success and happiness far from her so-called husband, and if he were to present himself, even just to explain himself, he would only cause her more suffering and heartache.

All he could do was appreciate her from afar.

"Well, what did you think?" Uncle Kelvin asked him, as they left the theatre. "Worth all the fuss about it?"

"Yes," Daniel said. "Definitely. I would rather like to see it again."

"High praise indeed," Uncle Kelvin said. "I rather think you'll struggle to get the tickets."

But Daniel knew he would go to any length if he could just see Isabella in her element on stage again.

CHAPTER 17

Daniel returned to the theatre as often as he could. He would have returned every night if he had been able, but Uncle Kelvin had been right. All of London was talking about this wonderful new play and its dazzling lead actress, and she performed to a full house every night. Often, Daniel went to the theatre even without a ticket, just to see the crowd pouring in through the doors and smile sadly as he watched Isabella's success from afar.

He had no more interest in other entertainment. He made excuses to Uncle Kelvin to escape plays and museums and gaming nights, and always returned to Isabella's theatre instead. At first, Uncle Kelvin accepted his excuses with good nature, and then began to tease Daniel about his obsession – perhaps he had feelings for that beautiful young actress, hm?

Finally, after several weeks of this, Uncle Kelvin lost his patience. "Really, my boy," he said. "There are other performances and other plays. What has you so obsessed with this one? Your fixation is becoming unhealthy."

Daniel opened his mouth to deny it, but instead he found

tears springing to his eyes. He could not bear to hide the truth any longer. "The star of the play is my wife," he said.

Uncle Kelvin stared at him as though he was trying to understand what Daniel had said. "Your— your wife?" he repeated, like his ageing ears may have misheard the word.

Daniel nodded. "I have been unfair to you, Uncle Kelvin," he said heavily. "I have come to stay with you, and infringed upon your hospitality, but I never told you *why* I am here in London, instead of home in Liverpool with mother and the business. I was married, yes. I still am married, technically, I suppose. But mother did not approve of her, and she schemed against me to be rid of her. If you heard the things she has done, Uncle, you would not believe it. It hardly sounds like real life. But it is true, all of it. I lost my wife, and I thought I would never see her again. And now she is here, on that stage, and she is performing *our* story. The play is based upon our lives, Uncle Kelvin. How could I stay away?"

Uncle Kelvin was quiet for a long while, looking at Daniel and considering his words. They must have been difficult to accept. "But why have you not approached her," Uncle Kelvin said eventually, "if she is your wife?"

"She will not want to see me," Daniel said. "Not after everything that happened. Her life is better without me." He shook his head. "Please, Uncle Kelvin. Do not ask any more. It hurts to speak of it."

But Uncle Kelvin hated to see his nephew so morose. Daniel had been excellent company for him, over the past several weeks, and if his mother had seen fit to ruin his life, it seemed fitting that his mother's brother should be the one to help repair it. Nothing would ever change, he thought ruefully, if left in the hands of these sentimental young folk, who spoke of revolution for society but were always so afraid to pursue their own personal, emotional fulfilment. If his nephew was forced to come face to face with his beautiful wife, and his wife finally discovered the truth, then surely things would change. All they would need is a push.

Which is how Uncle Kelvin ended up at the Brockhurst Theatre during the day, seeking an audience with the theatre company's owner. Madam Francine Majors was a force of nature, and he immediately knew that she was not a soul to be trifled with. Still, Uncle Kelvin did not think the truth would suffice here. The trick would be to force the pair to face one another. So instead, he enquired with Madam Majors about hiring the company for a private performance at his own estate.

Madam Majors was reluctant, considering how popular and successful her performance was proving, but Uncle Kelvin had the money to tempt her, and soon it was agreed: in two weeks' time, Isabella and the rest of the cast would arrive at Uncle Kelvin's estate and perform for his nephew and his friends.

Uncle Kelvin would not tell Daniel the entire truth, of course, or the plan would be ruined. He simply told Daniel that he had hired a theatre company for an evening's entertainment, and that his nephew's presence was expected. After all that Uncle Kelvin had done for Daniel, the boy could hardly refuse.

MEANWHILE, at the theatre, Isabella prepared for an exciting night's performance at a private estate. Madam Francine told her that their patron was a man named Mr Kelvin Sumner, a very well-to-do elderly gentleman who was a known supporter of the arts within the city. The play was already a huge success, but Madam Francine hoped that this additional attention from such a wealthy man and his theatre-loving associates might lead to greater opportunities – money to renovate the theatre, perhaps, or even to advance into a larger one. Isabella could not deny that that was exciting, but she was just as intrigued to see the estate that such a man might live in. It was set to be a very glamorous night.

She wished she could bring Tabitha and Abigail with her to see it as well, but Madam Francine insisted that it should be performers only, so Isabella left her sisters at the theatre, promising to tell them every detail as soon as she returned. Although time in the workhouse had left the sisters underfed and unwell, the time since had strengthened them again. They had been so relieved to be out of the workhouse and to have a glimmer of hope for the future that they had hardly minded squeezing into the tiny attic room above the theatre to sleep, and had gladly run errands for Madam Francine. Once the play became a success, Isabella's deal seemed even more wonderful than it had before, as her cut of the profits finally allowed them nice clothes and food of their own again. Isabella still insisted that they remain about the theatre for as long as they could, because she had seen how quickly savings could disappear when faced with misfortune, but one day soon they knew they would have a home together again.

Perhaps, if this rich new patron was particularly pleased with her play, they might manage that sooner rather than later.

So it was with high spirits and no small amount of excitement that Isabella arrived at Mr Sumner's estate with Madam Francine and the rest of the theatre company. They were welcomed by servants, and then shown out to the garden, where an outdoor stage had been erected. It was summer, so the sun would not disappear for many hours yet, but the hazy late-evening sunlight added a magical air to the set, and Isabella could not wait to begin the show.

Madam Francine introduced her to Mr Sumner, and Isabella found that she liked the older gentleman immediately. He had a lively glint in his eye, like he was both amused and delighted by all he saw, and his face had a warmth to it that suggested true kindness beneath.

THE ORPHAN STAR OF THE DOCKYARD

"Ah," Mr Sumner said, after introductions had been made. "You must meet my nephew, Daniel." He gestured across the garden, and Isabella looked, only mildly interested. Then she froze. There was no mistaking what she saw. Her husband stood not thirty feet away from her, clutching a wine glass, staring at her as though she were a ghost.

Isabella could hardly think. She absentmindedly offered him a curtsey, and then quickly made her excuses, claiming she needed to prepare for the performance. Her head was spinning. How could Daniel be here? Had he known she would be attending? Had he planned this? Or was it truly his uncle's innocent doing, a complete coincidence that they were both here? Daniel had never truly loved Isabella, of that she was certain, so she could easily believe that he might not only be here in London but also invite a theatre group to his home without noticing Isabella presence. Or perhaps he had known about her role, and he had not cared enough to contradict his uncle. Their marriage was two years in the past now, and Daniel had never respected it in the first place. Perhaps he was simply mocking her.

"I don't know if I can do it," Isabella said to Madam Francine, when the older woman found her again. "I find I am taken quite unwell."

"Nonsense, girl," Madam Francine said. "We have been paid a pretty penny to perform tonight, and you were perfectly fine not five minutes ago."

Isabella shook her head. "That man," she said softly, "Mr Sumner's nephew. He is my husband."

Madam Francine's eyes widened. Over their months of working together, Isabella had confided in her little pieces of her past, and the unspecified but heart breaking betrayal of her husband had been one of them. Madam Francine looked sympathetic, but she shook her head. "You must perform, my dear," she said. "Tonight is a great opportunity for all of us. For you as well. Do not allow this man to have any more control over your life."

Isabella wanted to argue, but she knew that Madam Francine was right. She would not allow Daniel to ruin this for her as well.

It felt strange, though, to perform her own story before the one person who would recognise the truth of it. She felt the emotions were even closer to the surface, and her voice shook with emotion as she sang, tears streaming down her face. The audience seemed enraptured, and Isabella did all she could to avoid looking at Daniel even once. She wanted him to experience this play, to marvel at her performance, to know how he had hurt her and how she had overcome it. She wanted him to see her success, and then she never wanted to see him again.

As soon as the performance was over and she had taken her bows, Isabella left for home without a single word to anyone.

CHAPTER 18

Daniel was furious with Uncle Kelvin for the trick that he had pulled, and had no qualms in telling him so. Uncle Kelvin seemed disappointed that the evening had not ended with a reconciliation between Daniel and Isabella, and Daniel had to tell him again that Isabella did not want to see him, and likely never would. He could not even go to the theatre now, he thought, because Isabella would know to look for him. She would surely tell others at the theatre that he was a scoundrel, at the very least, and have him refused entry.

If nothing else, at least Daniel now knew for certain that Isabella wanted nothing to do with him. It was a relief, in a way, to have his suspicions confirmed, and to know he was acting rightly by staying away.

So it was with some surprise that he heard from the servants that a Madam Francine Majors had come to pay a call on him and his uncle, and was desperately seeking an audience with them. "She would not take no for an answer, sir," the maid said. "I told her it was late, and she said it was no matter. She said you would want to speak to her."

"She's right," Daniel said. "We do." The hairs on the back of his neck stood on end as he hurried down to the drawing room. Why would she be here, calling on him, unless something were terribly wrong?

His fears were confirmed the moment he saw Madam Majors. Daniel had had little interaction with the woman that day at the party, but he had seen enough to know that she was a bold, no-nonsense sort of woman, quick to state her opinion and very difficult to rattle. But she looked beyond rattled now. Her hair was wild around her face, like she had run her hands through it too many times to count, and her eyes were wild.

"She is gone," Madam Majors said, as soon as Daniel and his uncle entered the room.

"Isabella?" Daniel asked. "She ran away?"

Madam Majors shook her head. "She has been taken," she said simply. Daniel stared at her, and she pulled a note out of her pocket and held it out to him. "Kidnapped. They are demanding more money than the theatre brings in, in a year for her return."

"I will pay it," Uncle Kelvin said at once. "No matter the sum."

Madam Majors shook her head. "That will not be enough," she said. "I believe she has been targeted. We are all aware of her connection to this family, yes?" Daniel and Uncle Kelvin nodded dumbly. "Before she joined my company, Isabella worked for another theatre owner, Mr Arnold Banker. She has not told me everything about her time with him, but she has told me enough. He threatened to ruin her, and I believe he tried to kill her once before. He certainly had her driven out of her friend's home and into the workhouse with lies. He must be behind this. I will not see money go to that man. And if we pay him, he will only hurt her again. We need to find her, and find the kidnappers. We need *proof*."

Daniel's head spun with fear. Isabella was in trouble. Isabella could be dead, for all anyone knew. But Uncle Kelvin remained level-headed, and got directly to the point. "Mr Banker," he said. "He was an acquaintance of your father, Daniel, wasn't he?"

"Yes," Daniel said, without thinking. "But my father is dead."

"Yes, yes, I am aware of that," Uncle Kelvin said. "But you must have known *other* people of Mr Banker's acquaintance, if he was known to your father, mustn't you?"

"Mrs Austin," Daniel said, thinking hard. "She may know him."

"Mrs Austin," Madam Majors repeated. "That was the name of the friend who turned her out of her house on Mr Banker's advice."

"Mrs Austin threw Isabella out?" Daniel was horrified.

Madam Majors nodded. "She introduced her to Mr Banker, got her work with him, and then threw her from the house after Mr Banker began to spread rumours about Isabella to ruin her. Seems unlikely she'll help us against him."

"No," Daniel said. "You're wrong." He had known Mrs Austin his entire life. She had been the one to arrange his marriage to the perfect woman in the first place, for goodness sake! She was a good woman at heart. It pained him to think that she had hurt Isabella, that she had caused Isabella to end up at the *workhouse*, but if Mrs Austin knew the truth, she would have to feel compelled to help. Her guilt over believing lies about the wonderful Isabella would be motivation enough, and if she found out that one of her friends was truly a villain, she would not stand for it, Daniel was certain.

"We must see Mrs Austin," Daniel said. "She may know what to do."

Mrs Austin, it turned out, had already retired for the night by the time they arrived, but Daniel would not allow that to delay him when Isabella's life was in danger. He pounded on the door, ignoring the maid's pleas to leave or she would be forced to fetch the police, demanding that they speak to Mrs Austin at once. He identified himself, and told the maid to tell her that Isabella was in grave danger, and only she could help. Five minutes later, Daniel, Uncle Kelvin and Madam Majors were situated in Mrs Austin's drawing room, while Mrs Austin sat opposite them, wrapped in a dressing gown with her hair up in rags. She listened intently as Daniel and Madam Majors each told their part in the story.

"The workhouse!" Mrs Austin exclaimed, her hand flying up to cover her mouth. "But she earned good money with Mr Banker. I thought she would find a house of her own with her income, not end up there."

"Isabella probably thought so too," Daniel said gently, "but she had a powerful man scheming against her."

"I should have known Isabella would never do the things that Arnold claimed," Mrs Austin said, with tears in her eyes. "I should have known it. But I did not see a single reason why he would lie. He is a villain."

"The past doesn't matter right now," Madam Majors said. "What matters is finding Isabella, before he can hurt her any more than he already has. Do you have any idea where he might be hiding her? Any property that he owns?"

"He owns several properties," Mrs Austin said. "But he would not keep her at the theatre. It would be too public and obvious." She frowned in thought. "He keeps a warehouse," she said. "On the Thames. It is small, and he was thinking of converting it for some other use, but he has not done so yet, so it must be quiet. I don't know where it is, precisely, but—"

"That will be enough," Uncle Kelvin said gently. "We can go

to the police, and they will be able to find out. We cannot thank you enough for your help."

Mrs Austin was crying. "I am just so sorry that I helped bring her to this," she said. "Please, find her. Bring her home safe."

"I will," Daniel said. "I swear it."

CHAPTER 19

Isabella lay on the cold stone floor, her thoughts swimming. She knew she was fading in and out of consciousness, and part of her was vaguely aware that that was a very bad sign, but she could not muster the energy to fight it or care.

Her legs were agony, but despite the pain, she could not regret her attempt to escape. The men had jumped at her outside her own theatre and knocked her unconscious with some harsh-smelling chemical pressed to her nose and mouth, and when she had first awakened, she had felt too heavy to move. Instead, she had pretended to still be unconscious, and listened to her attackers discussing in low voices what to do with her next. She heard Mr Banker's name, and she suppressed a groan. Of course he was the one who had organised this. He had told her he would ruin her, and instead she had succeeded beyond anything that Mr Banker had himself achieved.

She had needed to get out of there, as soon as she could, before Mr Banker arrived and finished what he had failed to do the night her cottage burned to the ground. She waited until her attackers were out of the room, distracted with some other conversation, and then she hauled herself to her feet, ready to run. She did not recognise anything about the place around her, and the sky outside the grimy windows had been dark, but she had stumbled towards them, hoping she might escape that way. The world still spun from whatever they had used to knock her unconscious. She struggled to focus, and she was finding it a little hard to breathe, but she knew running was her only chance.

She had not been quiet enough. Her attackers had heard her, and they had punished her for her attempt. Isabella had screamed in agony as they brought something heavy down on her legs, and the unconsciousness that overwhelmed her was a welcome relief from the pain. At least a day must have passed since then, and Isabella thought vaguely that she must be feverish, and that did not bode well for her survival. Mr Banker must want her alive for the present, though, or they would have broken more than her legs when she attempted to flee.

At this point, she almost wished they would kill her. Her legs were in constant agony, and her head pounded too, like someone was driving a nail between her eyes. But she could not give up. She could not fight, she thought, but she could not give up, not when her sisters were out there and needed her. Not when she had survived so much already.

She tried to sit up, but her body would not listen to her commands. She let out a soft groan, and heard one of her attackers chuckle from across the room. Tears stung Isabella's eyes. She would not give up. But her body felt so heavy, and her thoughts so unclear.

Soon, she would try to run again. Soon. Now, the pain was too much, and unconsciousness claimed her once again.

Mr Banker's warehouse was a run-down, relatively small building on the banks of the Thames. As soon as Daniel laid eyes on it, he began to run. The police shouted after him to stop, but Daniel did not listen. He could not bear to wait another second longer while his wife was in danger. He knew, in his heart, that she was somewhere inside those grim walls.

Isabella *had* to be all right. She had to be. He would never, never forgive himself if she was hurt.

The night was surprisingly cold for the season, and the moon was bright, illuminating Daniel's path. He burst through the doors of the warehouse without hesitating, and looked around in the darkness. A single light shone from a room at the top of the stairs, like a lamp.

Daniel tore after it.

He took in the room in a single glance. Two men sat near the entrance playing cards, their game lit by an oil lamp balanced on the table between them. One of them shouted in surprise when Daniel emerged, but he was no longer looking at them. On the other side of the room, laying on the cold floor, was Isabella. Her hair was plastered to her forehead with sweat, and she was shifting restlessly, as though trapped in some nightmare inside her head. She had a black eye and blood around her lips, but the most terrifying sight was her legs. They were both bent at unnatural angles, and Daniel could have sworn he saw a bit of bone poking out of her right calf. The sight would have been enough to make him sick, if he had not been so enraged instead. As the police ran in and shouted behind him, Daniel spun around and punched one of the kidnappers in the face, sending him skidding backwards. The other lunged for him, but Daniel punched him too, made strong by rage and desperation.

The police barrelled into the room after him and seized the struggling men, and Daniel raced to Isabella's side. She was unconscious, moaning in her sleep, and when Daniel pressed a hand to her forehead, he felt that she was burning up with fever.

He wanted to take her up in his arms and carry her away from this place, but he couldn't risk jolting her twisted legs. Instead, he took her hand in his and sat by her side, murmuring reassuring nothings until the doctor arrived.

THE PROCESS of moving Isabella to Uncle Kelvin's house was agony for them both. She let out a gasp of pain every time the carriage jolted beneath her, and Daniel could do nothing for her except squeeze her hand again and promise her that it would be over soon. He could not bear to have her out of his sight, lest something happen to her again. As soon as she was safely in bed at Uncle Kelvin's home, Daniel sent Mrs Austin to fetch her sisters from the theatre, but Daniel remained at the edge of Isabella's bed. The doctor had hope that her legs would heal, as long as she got the proper rest she needed, but he was concerned about the fever that had filled her. Daniel insisted that she was a fighter, and would not let the brutality of ruffians defeat her, but the doctor warned for caution. He was hopeful that she would recover, but he was far from certain.

Isabella had constant visitors after that, although she was not aware of it. Mrs Austin, Madam Francine, her sisters and Uncle Kelvin all kept her company through her fever, and Daniel never once left her side. The police were forced to interview him at his wife's bedside, where they informed him that the kidnappers had exposed Mr Banker as the mastermind behind the plot. He would not trouble Isabella any longer.

CHAPTER 20

Isabella first stirred three days after her rescue. Her eyelids fluttered open, and Tabitha leapt to her side at once. She helped Isabella to sit up slightly and drink a little water, but Isabella soon fell back asleep. Daniel was in such awe of her waking that he did not dare to approach her, lest his presence startle her, and Isabella did not seem conscious enough to realise she was in a strange room with her ex-husband standing in the corner. The next two times she awoke were the same.

When Isabella finally came back to herself, her head was sore and her limbs felt heavy, but her thoughts were clear for the first time in days. She drifted to consciousness, taking in the softness of the sheets around her and the beam of sunlight that fell across her face, and then her memories flooded back to her. The men who attacked her on the street. The warehouse. Her attempt to escape, and the agony in her legs.

She sat up with a jerk, her heart racing. She was sitting in an unfamiliar room, but it did not look like part of the warehouse. It was richly appointed, with red velvet curtains hanging around the window frame and a plush carpet on the floor. The dressing table was relatively sparse, but the silver-coated hairbrush and hand mirror left there suggested they belonged to someone of some wealth. Isabella pressed a hand to her throbbing head. Her arm was bruised, but intact. Remembering her legs, she pulled the blankets up to look at them. The parts she could see were a mass of bruises, and her calves were both hidden behind plaster. She did not dare to try and move them.

"The doctor believes you will be able to walk again," a familiar voice said, "but you need to rest for a few weeks to be sure."

She dropped the blankets and looked up. Daniel was sitting in a corner of the room, half-concealed by the fall of the curtains. Her heart began to race. "What are you doing here?" she asked. "Where am I?"

"You're at Uncle Kelvin's," Daniel said softly. "Where you performed. We did not think it would be safe for you to return to the theatre. Your sisters are here too, but they are both resting."

"No," Isabella said. She tried to move her legs to climb out of bed, and pain shot through them. She gasped, and Daniel was at her side at once, taking her hand. She pulled away. "I can't stay here."

"Please," Daniel said. "You'll hurt yourself. You need rest."

"I need rest?" she shouted. "And do you know why I need rest, Mr Kimble? It is because of the hurt that you have done me!"

"I know it," Daniel said, "and I am truly sorry for what I have done. But please, you cannot move. I will fetch your sisters if you do not wish me here."

"I will not impose on your uncle's hospitality," Isabella said. "What did you tell him? That I was your errant wife?"

"I told him that I lost you," Daniel said. "That I had no chance to find you and make amends."

"You need feel no accountability towards me, Mr Kimble," Isabella said. "You made it clear from the very beginning that I am not truly your wife. I can be of no use to you now, so you need not worry yourself. I will find somewhere else to convalesce."

"You *are* truly my wife!" he said desperately.

"You did not show it," Isabella said. "Why should I believe anything you wish to say to me now?"

"Because I love you!" Daniel shouted.

Isabella stared at him, too shocked by his outburst to speak. She could feel tears forming in her eyes, the old heartbreak ripped anew. "If this is how you show love, Mr Kimble," she said, "you do not know what love truly is. Did you instruct your uncle to invite the company to perform here? Have you been following me? Is that your *love*?"

"No," Daniel said. He reached for her hand again, but she pulled hers away. "Believe me, Isabella. I found you by accident. My uncle wished to see the most popular new show in town, and when I saw you on stage, dazzling the crowd, I could hardly believe it. I did not wish to interrupt your new life, but when I told my uncle who you were, he thought he was doing good by trying to reunite us."

"You cannot have told your uncle what you did," Isabella said, "if he thought reintroducing us would help anything."

"Isabella," Daniel said desperately, "I never betrayed you. I am truly sorry for what happened, but it was all a scheme by my mother. I would never hurt you like that. I love you, Isabella."

Isabella stared at him, her eyes filling with tears. How could she believe him? She wanted his words to be true, but she had seen him lying there with Clare with her own eyes. He had spoken sweet words to her before, and she had believed him, but the truth was in his actions, was it not? She shook her head to try and clear the tears as Tabitha burst through the door into the room.

"Izzy!" she said. "You're awake." She rushed forward and took Isabella in her arms. Then she turned to Daniel. "You're upsetting her," she hissed.

"I'm trying to explain," Daniel said, but Tabitha cut him off.

"No," she said. "You heard the doctor. She cannot be distressed. Please leave, and give her some peace."

Daniel looked as though he wished to argue, but then he glanced at Isabella again and nodded. With a small bow towards his wife, he departed.

"Oh, Izzy," Tabitha said, holding her sister tighter in her arms. "We were so worried about you. We didn't know if you would wake. How are you feeling?"

"Sore," Isabella said softly. "But alive."

"Thank heavens," Tabitha said. "When Madam Francine found that ransom note—I thought we'd lost you, Isabella. But Mr Kimble suggested we speak to Mrs Austin, and she knew where he might be keeping you at once."

"Mrs Austin?" Isabella asked.

"Oh, yes," Tabitha said. "She was heartbroken when she found out what had become of us, and how Mr Banker had manipulated her. She wanted us all to return to her house and rest there, but Mr Kimble insisted that you come here, and he is still officially your husband, so his demands won out. His Uncle Kelvin has been terribly nice to us, and Mr Kimble has barely left your side."

"Why would he care?" Isabella asked. "He is the one who betrayed me."

"I know, Izzy," Tabitha said. "But I am starting to believe there may have been some mistake. He found you himself, you know. He ran into the warehouse where they kept you and fought the men there. It all sounded very gallant. And he has been beside himself with worry for you ever since. I don't understand it. He simply said he needed to speak to you about it, and prayed that you would wake."

"I don't know what he could say," Isabella said, "that would make any of this better." But she remembered how Daniel had looked at her, the fervour with which he had declared his love. Perhaps he had a strange, dishonest understanding of the feeling. Or perhaps he was not lying, and his mother truly had hatched some scheme.

But Isabella's head hurt very much, and the pain in her legs was growing too. She was not in a state to risk heartache again.

"We have to go to Mrs Austin's," Isabella said. "As soon as we can."

Tabitha nodded. "But please stay here for a little longer," she said. "It was terrible moving you here. If they move you again, I think your legs may not recover. Gain a little strength first, and then we will go."

And although Isabella hated the thought of accepting anything else from Daniel or his relatives, she was forced to agree.

CHAPTER 21

Daniel did not return to Isabella's room for the next several days, although Tabitha confided in her that he asked after her constantly. Isabella continued to sleep off the rest of the fever, and in her waking moments, she was visited by her sisters and by a tearful and deeply remorseful Mrs Austin. Madam Francine was as no-nonsense as always, telling Isabella that the story was in all the papers, and that tickets for the show starring Isabella's understudy were even more popular than they had ever been, netting Isabella extra money while she slept. When Isabella was ready to return to the stage, she promised, she would be an absolute sensation.

Even Daniel's Uncle Kelvin visited for a short while, inquiring after her health and bringing her the evening paper to read. She thanked him for it, but she felt so awkward in his presence, knowing she was relying on his hospitality but hardly believing she deserved it, that she managed to say little else to him.

As the days passed, she thought more and more about Daniel's absence. Her dismissal of him had been absolute, but she found herself wishing she could see him and speak to him again. She knew she was a fool for fostering any sort of hope regarding him, but she could not stop thinking about his words when she had first awakened, the intense passion with which he had told her he loved her, the avowal that he had never meant to betray her, that his mother had been scheming against them.

Finally, she screwed up her courage and asked Tabitha to ask him to visit, if he could spare the time. Daniel appeared almost immediately, looking terribly nervous. As he entered the room, she took the time to properly consider him. He looked thinner than she remembered, and he had dark circles under his eyes, like stress and lack of sleep had both taken their toll. He was still handsome, she thought, but there was a deep sadness around him that he had not carried before.

"Isabella," he said softly.

"Are you well?" she asked. She could not decide whether she should call him Daniel or Mr Kimble, so she omitted the name altogether.

"I am better," he said, "now you are safe. And you?"

"I'm healing," she said. She fidgeted with the embroidery on the bed cover. "My sister tells me I have you to thank for my rescue. Thank you."

"I wish I could have done more," Daniel said. "I wish I could have found you sooner."

"The fact that you found me at all is—" She did not know what to say. How could you express your gratitude for being alive in words? "Thank you. I am in your debt."

"You could never be in my debt," Daniel said. "I will be working to make amends with you for the rest of my life."

Isabella looked away, towards the window. She was afraid to ask him what she really wanted to know. Even after several years, the heartache was too raw. "What happened that day?" she said eventually. "When I found you? What is the truth?"

"You were right," Daniel said slowly. "My mother wanted me to marry Clare Swindon, and she would do anything to make it happen. She drugged me, Isabella. Then Clare climbed into bed beside me and waited for you to return from your outing with my mother, so you would catch her accidentally and think I had betrayed you. There are men at home who can confirm this. Solicitors who overheard my mother and Clare discussing the plot. And the servants will tell you as well that Clare never came to the house at my invitation while you were not present. I swear to you, Isabella. There has never been anyone else."

Isabella considered him. His face was open and honest, desperate to make her understand. He did not look like a man trying to deceive. Before the horror of that day, hadn't she always thought Daniel was a strikingly honest man, the kind that you could trust?

"Why didn't you try to find me," Isabella asked softly, "if that is the truth?"

"I did," he said. "I wrote to Mrs Austin twice to enquire about your whereabouts, but she did not reply. She must have thought it for the best."

"It was," Isabella said. "She never told me you wrote, but… I did not want to see you."

"And then, once I found out the truth of what my mother had done, I could not bear to try and drag you back there to be hurt again. I thought you would have a better life, without me, Isabella. And you did! You are the star of London."

"The star of London," Isabella snapped back, "who was kidnapped by a jealous ex-employer who ruined my life because I refused to become his mistress. The star of London who lived in a workhouse and nearly died in a fire and barely survived to see that day!"

Daniel had tears in his eyes. "I would spend the rest of my life making amends with you," he said, "if that is what it took. If you would let me."

But Isabella did not know what to say. Her heart wanted her to take Daniel in her arms, hold him tight and promise that they would never be parted again. But her head had seen the cruelty of this world, and it would not allow her to be rash.

"Please stay, at least," Daniel said. "Don't go to Mrs Austin's. Recover here."

That was an easier request. "Yes," Isabella said. "All right. I can do that."

Daniel visited Isabella every day after that. He scoured London's bookshops for all the latest and most exciting stories, and the pair read them together, like they used to do. Daniel brought flowers too, all the bright blooms that he could find, until Isabella's room overflowed with them. But what Isabella valued most was his company. Her recovery was long, but as the weeks passed, she gradually got to know her husband again, and this time there was no misunderstanding between them. Slowly, she told him all that had happened to her since she had fled to London, and even details about her life before she met him, her memories of her mother and father. In return, Daniel told her how he had discovered the truth about his mother, and how he had come to London to escape her. Every day, Isabella felt the warmth of her affection growing. They could not erase the past, but as they discussed it together, Isabella thought that maybe it could be forgiven.

And Daniel was not the only member of the household that she grew to appreciate. Uncle Kelvin brought her the paper every evening, and soon the pair of them fell into an easy friendship, discussing plays and theatre and all the gossip of London society. Uncle Kelvin vowed that he would take her to see every worthwhile production in London as soon as she was recovered, and Isabella realised that this is what had been missing in her previous life with Daniel. Even if Daniel had loved her, she had lacked acceptance from the world around him, and that feeling of judgement had worried her sick. Now all she felt was love and appreciation from every corner, and for the first time in her life, she truly knew what it was to feel safe.

In this setting, bit by bit, with her friends around her, Isabella opened her heart to Daniel again.

And then, one day, his mother came to call.

CHAPTER 22

The knock at the door of Uncle Kelvin's house was not unexpected that Friday afternoon. Both Mrs Austin and Madam Francine were frequent visitors, and Madam Francine was eager to begin to work on a new script with Isabella, now that she was feeling better. Isabella was already sitting at the pianoforte, testing the pedals with delicate pushes of her still-healing legs. She could walk again, but it had been a difficult and painful process, and she still tired very quickly and needed to rest. She could play without using the pedals, of course, but she tried to exercise her legs in every gentle way she could. She was determined to recover and be as strong as before. She would not allow Mr Banker to leave even the slightest spectre over her life.

When Isabella heard the knock, she rose slowly, moving over to the armchair. Daniel sat nearby, reading a book, and he looked up and smiled when he saw her approaching. He took her hand and kissed it tenderly, and she settled beside him, full of that calm anticipation that precedes the visit of a friend who you know accepts you for precisely who you are.

Then she heard the sharp sound of Mrs Kimble's voice

slicing through the air. "Where is my son?" she was saying to the maid who answered the door. "I know he is here. Show me to him."

Isabella sat up straighter, wanting to run, and Daniel took her hand again and squeezed it reassuringly. Then he stood, ready to face his mother.

"Daniel!" she said, as she entered the room. The maid curtsied behind her, looking terrified, and scurried away. "There you are." Her eyes slid over to focus on Isabella. "I would ask you what you are doing, dallying in London, but it seems I have found my answer. You are reunited with your wife at last."

"With no thanks to you," Daniel said. "What is it you want, Mother?"

"Is that any way to speak to the woman who raised you?" Mrs Kimble said.

"The business is suffering," she said. "Your father entrusted it to *you*, and it needs you present to prosper. Instead, you choose to gallivant around London with a woman who abandoned you and who had no place in your life in the first place, and let your father's legacy turn to dust!"

"The only thing I value about father's legacy," Daniel said, "is that his ridiculous marriage clause brought Isabella and I together. I have no interest in the shipping business if it is tied to you and Clare Swindon and all of your cruelty and manipulation."

"Cruelty?" Mrs Kimble repeated. "I have only ever acted in your best interests, Daniel, regardless of how resistant you have been to considering them."

"Do you honestly believe that, sister?" Uncle Kelvin had appeared in the doorway. He was considering his sister with a stern expression on his face.

"Kelvin!" Mrs Kimble said. "I'm glad to see you. I don't know what my son has told you about his reasons for being here, but I must insist you send him home. We are all suffering without him."

"I cannot do that," Uncle Kelvin said. "Daniel has told me exactly why he is here, and what you have done to both him and his dear wife. Did you really believe I would let that stand? If I were to have my way, we would inform the law of your behaviour. See how your society in Liverpool likes *that*. But Daniel is a gentler soul than I, and he has refused. He simply wishes to be left in peace with his wife."

"His *wife*," Mrs Kimble said. "He hasn't seen her in years. How can she be considered his wife?"

"He hasn't seen her in years," Uncle Kelvin said, "because of *your* schemes. You are lucky I do not call the constable this very moment."

Isabella rose shakily to her feet. "Mrs Kimble," she said. "I know you have never liked me or accepted me. I did my very best to live up to your standards, but nothing pleased you. You have caused me and my husband both great harm. But I can promise you, you will never have power over my life again."

"Nor mine," Daniel said. "I will not be returning to Liverpool, Mother. I cannot trust that you will not attempt to ruin things in my life again, and if I have any chance of being reunited with my wife, I will not risk inflicting your meddling on her again. You may find someone else to care for my inheritance. I do not want Kimble Freighters, nor anything else you have to offer."

"Daniel," Mrs Kimble said. She stepped closer. "You do not know what you are saying. This girl has bewitched you."

"He is perfectly in charge of his faculties," Uncle Kelvin said. "In fact, I think we are both seeing clearly around you for the very first time. You may see yourself out."

Mrs Kimble gaped at the pair of them. But Uncle Kelvin was already guiding her out of the room, towards the door. He stopped on the other side of it and watched his sister depart.

"Are you all right?" Daniel asked Isabella, once the front door closed again, and he was certain his mother had gone. Isabella nodded. "Do you really mean it?" she said. "You would give up your inheritance for me?"

"I would do anything for you," he said.

"But—your inheritance is the only reason you wished to marry in the first place."

"Then it has already served its purpose," Daniel said. "It brought me to you." He gently took her hand and raised it to his lips, pressing a respectful kiss against her knuckles. Isabella smiled, her heart so warm and full she thought it might burst, and stepped closer to press her lips to his.

CHAPTER 23

"How would you feel," Daniel said to Isabella one morning, a few days later, "about America?"

"How would I feel about America?" Isabella repeated. "How do you mean? As a country? Do you wish to take a trip?" She knew little about the country, beyond what she had read in novels, but ships often departed for its shores, both from Liverpool and from the Thames, and Isabella had often watched them and thrilled to think of the great vessels travelling so far. America was a strange, hectic land, she thought, with strange, hectic habits, only recently settled from a great civil war waged to end slavery in all its lands. She could appreciate the idealism of the nation, fighting for independence from the British and rushing into modernity, exploring unexplored lands and creating new settlements, new cities, new lives. There was darkness in the nation too, she thought, and pain from a war that had ripped deep into its foundations and had not yet healed, but it was an exciting land of opportunity, where class could be forgotten and identities forged anew.

"Not a trip," Daniel said. "I was considering whether you might like to live there."

"*Live* there?" Isabella asked. Her heart began to beat wildly at the thought.

Daniel took both her hands in his. "You would be a sensation there," he said. "The starlet of London, come across the ocean. They would devour your plays. And we would be far from my mother's influence, and from all those stuffy work associates that dared to sneer at you before. We'd be in a country where we would be accepted and valued for who we are, not where we came from."

"It's so far," Isabella said. "What about my sisters and my friends?"

"If you would rather stay," Daniel said, "then we can stay. But it would be a new life for us. And I think you would be wonderful, Isabella. They would adore you."

"As long as *you* adore me," Isabella said jokingly, "then I am perfectly happy."

"Oh, I will always adore you," Daniel said. "But it would be selfish of me not to offer others the opportunity to also."

They did not discuss the matter again for another couple of days, but Isabella found herself thinking of it in her quiet moments. It would be a fresh start, she thought, a new beginning away from the ghosts of Mrs Kimble and Clare Swindon and Mr Banker and all the hurt that she had suffered. When no one else was around, she began searching the library for books about the country, devouring the words of Louisa May Alcott and her ilk, and scouring through the newspapers for reports on the country. Baedeker offered no guides for countries outside Europe, but she found herself pausing in bookshops, searching for anything that might inform her more about the great city of New York.

Eventually, she took her sisters aside and told them of her thoughts. To Isabella's delight and relief, they were both thrilled with the idea. They both adored the idea of a new adventure, they told her, and their greatest desire was to see their sister happy, after she had done so much for them.

Isabella planned to bring up the issue with Daniel in private again, but Abigail's excitement could not be tamed, and her youngest sister mentioned it that very afternoon, while they all sat in the garden with Uncle Kelvin and Madam Francine, taking afternoon tea.

"New York!" Uncle Kelvin said. "That's news to me, boy."

"And me as well," Daniel said. A grin spread across his face as he turned to his wife. "Does that mean you've changed your mind?" he asked. "You want to go?"

"I never said I didn't," Isabella said. "I just needed some time to think. Yes, I would very much like to go. But it will be difficult leaving behind our friends here."

"Who said anything about leaving anyone behind?" Uncle Kelvin said. "I assume family is invited, if your sisters are tagging along. I've always wanted to see New York."

"Do you mean it?" Isabella asked, her heart swelling.

"Certainly," Uncle Kelvin said. "I have grown rather fond of all of you. It would be far too dull and quiet in London here without you."

"I would be losing my great star," Madam Francine said. "To the glitz of New York!"

"Then perhaps, my dear Madam Francine," Uncle Kelvin said, "you should consider moving your company too. There are many opportunities in the new world, and Isabella is bound to become a star."

"Move the company?" Madam Francine repeated.

"Oh, they would love you there!" Abigail said enthusiastically. "Isabella won't want to move so far without you. She told me she would miss you terribly. And Isabella *is* your company, now, isn't she?"

"I wouldn't say that," Isabella said, "but it is true that I would miss you."

"I would say it," Madam Francine said, smiling. "You rescued my theatre from ruin, Isabella, and made us the talk of London instead. There is no company without you." She looked thoughtful for a moment. "Why ever not?" she said eventually. "I think we are all in need of a fresh start and a new adventure."

Isabella beamed.

The following weeks were a rush of activity, as Francine sold the theatre and the party of six arranged for their tickets and packed up their possessions. Uncle Kelvin, with his endless resourcefulness and theatre connections, spread the news that the famous Isabella Kimble was travelling to be a star in New York, and soon London was abuzz with it, in a way that Uncle Kelvin assured her meant people would be just as excited for her arrival on the other side of the Atlantic, and eager to engage the hottest new thing in town.

Two months after they first discussed it, Isabella, Daniel, Tabitha, Abigail, Uncle Kelvin and Madam Francine all climbed aboard a transatlantic steamer, with Mrs Austin there to wave them off. All the new innovations in steamship travel meant that the journey would take a mere nine days to complete, and the group spent much of the early days enjoying tours around the ship, admiring the engines and the ingenuity that made it fly across the sea. Isabella's pianoforte was in storage for the journey, but she found herself frequently on deck with her sisters, watching the dolphins dance around the prow of the ship and inventing light-hearted songs, like she used to do for Tabitha so many years ago. She felt full of joy and hope, and although the future was uncertain, she knew that she was safe in her family's love.

CHAPTER 24

They arrived in New York one day ahead of schedule, and Isabella stepped off the steamship into the sunny bustle of the city. Uncle Kelvin had already arranged accommodation for them all, and they spent the next several days exploring the island, marvelling at the accents and delighting in all the new shops and sights it had to offer. The park at the centre of the island offered particular joy, and Isabella imagined a beautiful future wandering its paths with her husband and sisters and friends around her, at peace with the world.

They soon learned that Uncle Kelvin's gossip campaign had worked splendidly. They merely had to mention Isabella's name and people smiled, excited to see the new sensation sure to take over the city. Madam Francine purchased an old warehouse, and together the friends worked to convert it into a theatre for Isabella's next great hit. The patrons of New York were already begging for a run of her previous play, and Isabella agreed to oblige them, but her heart was full of so many new dreams and emotions, and she was eager to weave them into something new.

Their opening night sold out almost as soon as they

announced it, and the money began to fly in. Once the theatre was up and running, Daniel began to think about new business ventures of his own, but the production was so successful that he did not need to worry. Daniel still made sure he attended every night, seated at the back where he could marvel at his wife unnoticed. She was captivating, he thought, and he was amazed that fate had brought him into her life, not just once, but twice. He had been given another chance with his beloved, and he would not let anything tear them apart again.

Uncle Kelvin quickly dove into New York society, attending every art showing and play he could. He brought Isabella with him when she was not performing, and her sisters when she was, and delighted in introducing everyone to his darling, talented nieces who had encouraged him to start a new adventure.

Several months after their arrival in New York, Daniel received a letter from his solicitor, informing him of his mother's death. He grieved for her, not as she was at the end of his life, but as he remembered her from when he was a child, but he could not deny he felt a certain relief that she would never threaten his happiness again. With her death, complete control of Kimble Freighters fell to Daniel, but Daniel had no intention of moving back to Liverpool and facing society there again. He purchased a few more warehouses and moved operations to New York, and the decision proved quite lucrative, providing funds to expand the theatre and put on ever more elaborate productions. Tabitha and Abigail joined Isabella on the stage and at the pianoforte, and their family productions became the stuff of legends. Everyone wished to meet the talented sisters who grew up in the slums of Liverpool and faced down sabotage, kidnap and attempted murder to bring their beautiful voices to the people of New York.

As for Daniel and Isabella, they were never separated again. They had finally found a world that loved and accepted them for who they were, and although they had their disagreements, as all couples do, they were delighted in one another's company and the future they could build together. Along with their many children, and then grandchildren, they lived in comfort and joy for the rest of their days, and they were always thought of fondly, as two people who understood the true meaning of happiness and of love.

THE ORPHAN DAUGHTER'S DILEMMA

TWO STEADFAST ORPHAN'S DREAMS:
PART II

CHAPTER 1

Six-year-old Ada Thompson sat atop a pile of hay in the barn, a cheap paperbound book in her lap. With her left hand, she stroked the soft wool of the lamb she had brought up onto the hay with her, while her right turned the pages.

"Ada?" her father called from the doorway of the born. "Are you in here?"

"I'm here, Papa," she said.

Ada's father was a relatively short man in his thirties with a freckled face and a broad smile. He'd lived on the farm he now owned since he was born, and had loved working with the animals almost ever since. It delighted him to see his daughter taking to the farm and the animals in the same way. Even at six, she had a natural talent and understanding for animals that made her father's heart swell with pride. But perhaps that was natural, because she had been helping her father on the farm almost as soon as she could toddle.

Ada's mother had been a kind and gentle woman, but she had died when Ada was only six months' old, and her father was almost overcome with grief. If he had not needed to care for baby Ada and all the animals on the farm, he might have succumbed to his grief, but Ada's father was driven onwards by a sense of love and duty for those around him. It was difficult for one man to care for both a baby and a farm full of animals while grieving, and his only solution had been to constantly keep baby Ada with him. She had grown up around the sheep and the cows and the chickens, learning to speak by chattering nonsense to them, learning to read while sitting with the calves in the barn. Now six, she had pretty blonde curls tied back with a ribbon, a pert nose, large blue eyes, and a small gap in her front teeth behind her smile.

Whenever Ada's father could not find her, he knew she would be squirrelled away somewhere with the animals, probably reading. Still, when he saw Ada there with the book in her lap, Ada's father's smile grew even wider. "How's the story?" he asked.

"It's wonderful, Papa!" Ada said. "Thank you!"

"Well," her father said. "Anything for my little girl."

At six years old, Ada had already mastered all of her letters, and her numbers too, and was constantly hungry for new things to read. Her own father had taught her all he knew of reading, which was little more than the letters themselves, using a slate and some chalk and a determination that his daughter would be as well-prepared for life as a poor farmer's daughter could be, but he had been amazed by how eagerly she had taken to learning.

The village had no school, and books were difficult to acquire, especially those that would be of interest to a child, but her father did what he could to provide for her. Everyone in the village knew that little Ada Thompson was a voracious reader, and the traders kept an eye out for anything that might interest her on their travels, selling it to her father for the cost they paid for it, out of respect for the man and his family.

Ada's eyes moved over the final page of the book, and then she closed it with a decisive snap. "Finished," she said.

"Already?" Her father sat down beside her and looked at the completed volume in her hands. "I only got it for you a few hours ago."

"I know," Ada said, "but it was good. I couldn't wait!" She grinned at him, hugging the book to her chest, and then paused as her face fell. She had finished her hard-won gift too quickly. Perhaps her Papa would think her ungrateful. "Don't worry, Papa," she added. "I'll read it again. And again and again."

Her Papa took the book from her hands and considered it. "This is beyond me, you know, Ada," he said. "I couldn't read so many big words. But Mr Lewis at the market promised me you'd like it."

"I did," Ada said. "I do! It's about a boy who wants to go on adventures, so he sneaks onto a sailing ship, and they're supposed to be travelling to the *Americas*, but there's a storm along the way, and—"

Ada's father smiled fondly and stroked Ada's hair as she talked. She was only six, but she'd already surpassed him in her penchant for learning. He had always found his letters so difficult, and he read in a halting way, without confidence or enjoyment. Ada seemed to devour knowledge, always hungry for more.

"I wish I could be as clever as you with book learning, Ada," he said. "You're far too smart for the likes of me."

"Did Mama like reading?" Ada asked, and her father looked away. His eyes lost both the shine and the focus they had had while she had been speaking of her book, and his smile slipped away. This happened every time Ada mentioned her mother.

"Your Mama was a very smart woman," he said after a moment, his eyes focussed on the wall of the barn as though taking in something that only he could see. "Smart in so many ways. But she never got the chance to learn to read."

"We could have taught her, Papa," Ada said. "I'm sure we could've."

"Mm," her Papa said, in distracted agreement. He seemed to snap out of his memories suddenly, and he stroked his daughter's hair again. "Maybe you could read the book to me," her Papa said. "If you don't mind reading it again."

Ada's face shone with happiness as he handed the book back to her. She shuffled in her seat rather importantly, searching for the perfect reading position, and then opened the book to the beginning again. "All right," she said. He wrapped an arm around her, pulling her close, as the lamb nosed at her side. "Here we go."

ADA COULD NOT REMEMBER her mother. She did miss her, when she thought about her, but her father was kind and warm-hearted, and Ada did not want for love. Her best friend, Betsy, lived only a ten-minute walk away, and she often came to the farm to keep Ada company and to help with the animals. The two girls had been born only a few weeks apart, and they had been in each other's lives ever since. Betsy's family was like a second family to Ada. Her father always had a smile and a joke for her, and her mother was always fussing over Ada when she saw her, demanding she take extra food for herself and bring snacks back to her Papa.

Still, Ada lived in fear of loss, knowing, without being able to articulate it, that anyone around her could be stolen from her with little warning. She cuddled close to her Papa and to Betsy every time she saw them, and at night she would pray to God to allow them to stay.

But although Ada could not imagine ever losing Betsy, Betsy, at seven years old, had bigger ambitions. One day, Ada and Betsy were sitting in the barn with the latest batch of new-born lambs, stroking their soft fleece and trading secrets in giggling whispers, when Betsy excitedly announced that she had news from her father. "He told me yesterday," Betsy said, "that when I'm eighteen, he's going to take me to *London*."

"London?" Ada asked. She had heard of the place. It was very far away, she knew, and where important people lived, like the Queen and her family.

"He has a friend there," Betsy said excitedly. "A rich old man. He says I'll be able to work for him."

"Work doing what?" Ada asked. She paused her hand over the lamb's fleece, a fear creeping into her heart that she could not put into words.

"I dunno," Betsy said. "Rich, city people work, I s'pose. Can you believe it, though? My Papa says that London is *very* big. He says it has more people in it than everyone in the village, including all the sheep and the cats and everything too."

Ada tried to imagine so many people all living in one place, but it seemed impossible. Betsy must have been mistaken, she decided.

"How does your Papa know him," Ada asked, "if he's so rich and so far away?"

Betsy shrugged. "Papa knows lots of people," she said. "Why wouldn't he know a rich man in London? Papa knows everyone." Betsy was grinning, but Ada could not hide the sadness from her face, and Betsy paused and frowned. "Aren't you excited, Ada?" she asked. "It's so far away!"

Ada ran her fingers through the lamb's fleece, not looking at her friend. "It's all right," she said. "It's just— I don't want you to go far away, Betsy. I want you to stay here with me."

"I won't go 'til I'm eighteen, silly," Betsy said. "That's so long away. That's—" She paused, frowning slightly as she tried to count. "Twelve years!"

That was true. It was twelve whole years away. Ada had only been alive six years in *total*. Betsy was not supposed to leave until two more whole lifetimes in the future. It was so far away it barely counted at all.

"And maybe you can come with me!" Betsy added. "I can't go without you."

Ada nodded, but she knew that would not happen. She would never want to go so far away from her Papa, and from all the animals and everyone she knew. Home was *here*, not London, wherever that might be. It was lucky, Ada thought, that eighteen was forever and ever away. Twelve years away was basically *never*, so she wouldn't worry about it at all.

Still, when Ada was getting ready for bed that night, she couldn't help mentioning Betsy's story to her Papa. "But I won't have to go far away," she said, "will I, Papa? I'll stay here with you."

"You can stay here as long as you want to," her Papa said, kissing her softly on the crown of her head. "But one day, you might want to leave too."

Ada shook her head. "I won't," she said. "I want to stay with you."

"Then you will stay," her Papa said, "and you and Betsy will write to each other, like the clever girls that you are. You'll tell her all about the animals and her Mama, and she can tell you about life in the big city, and I'm sure you'll both be happy."

This was good enough for Ada. She nodded and kissed her Papa on the cheek goodnight.

TWELVE YEARS LATER, Ada barely remembered the conversation she had once had with Betsy in the barn or her promise to her Papa afterwards. She remembered that Betsy would leave, of course, as Betsy had mentioned it several times since, but although her day of departure must surely come soon, Ada had managed to convince herself to be excited for her friend. Ada

THE ORPHAN DAUGHTER'S DILEMMA

would still never choose to leave her Papa — how could she, when there was so much work on the farm to be done? And when he had no one but her to care for him? — but she had accepted that her friend had different dreams. Sometimes, Ada even imagined leaving for London with her. Not with any seriousness, of course, but with the idle comfort of someone who knew such a thing would never *actually* happen, and so could let her fancy run wild on the subject. She imagined the city folk they would meet, and the things they would see. She imagined handsome men for both her and Betsy, men who would be struck by their country charms and be determined to woo them. In all her fancies, though, she never stayed in London for very long. The handsome men — who were both very rich and very kind as well, of course — would always dream of a quieter life, and they would all eventually return to the village, where Ada would teach her husband to care for the sheep and smile at him good naturedly when he got confused by a bridle or startled by the chickens, as a city boy was highly likely to do.

On the day of Ada's eighteenth birthday, Ada's Papa invited both Betsy and her father Frank around for a small, private celebration. Betsy's eighteenth birthday had already passed several weeks before, and Ada felt a sadness in her heart at the knowledge that her days with her life-long best friend were numbered. She was determined to enjoy the time that they had, however, and she had managed to put together quite a spread for the four of them, with jam sandwiches and delicious tea. Her father had a surprise for her too — a real cake, just big enough for the four of them to each have a slice. Betsy gifted Ada with a new ribbon for her hair, and Ada's father gave her a locket with a lock of hair inside, which he said had been her mother's. Ada was so overwhelmed by the gift that she cried, and everyone at the party huddled around her, hugging her tight and showing her their love.

But the party was interrupted by the sound of a loud, pained moan, coming from somewhere outside. Ada's father sat up straighter and listened, but Ada was already on her feet, running for the door. She was certain the noise had come from one of the cows — she recognised the timbre of the creature's voice — and she already knew in her heart that something terrible had happened. She scrambled to the barn, following the sound of pained moans, and found one of the cows lying collapsed on the ground, its eyes rolling.

"Oh, Minnie," Ada said, climbing over the division and rushing through the straw towards the fallen creature. "Minnie, what is the matter?"

Her father had reached the barn at this point, with Betsy and Frank not far behind him. The moment he saw the cow, he climbed over the fence too and crouched down beside her. He looked at Minnie's rolling eyes and the froth around her mouth, and then pulled back her lips to look inside. He pressed his hands down Minnie's back, while she moaned in protest.

"What's wrong with her, Papa?" Ada asked. Even after eighteen years on the farm, she had never seen anything like this.

Her father just shook his head. "We'd better move the other cows to the other barn," he said. "In case it's a catching illness. Then you should go run and heat up a pail of water," he said. "Might help with soothing her."

With Betsy and Frank's help, they moved all the other cows away from Minnie, and then Ada and Betsy ran to start a fire and heat up the water as her father had requested. "What's wrong with her?" Betsy murmured to Ada, as they worked. "Do you know?"

Ada shook her head. Death was a part of farm life. Animals died of sickness, animals died of old age, and animals were slaughtered to be eaten when the time was right. She had found animals dead in the barn before, creatures who had hidden their illness and died in the night without anyone there to witness it. She had cared for sick animals too, ever since she was small, and some of them had gotten better, and some of them had not. A sick cow should not have bothered her as much as it did. She always felt sadness when they lost one of them, especially a dairy cow like Minnie, who had a name and a character of her own and who was not expected to die. The loss of the milk would be a blow, of course, but the loss of Minnie herself would sting too. But it was expected. Animals got sick, just as people did. It was the way of nature. Yet she felt a chill in her bones now as she thought of Minnie's rolling eyes and the froth about her lips. There was something strange about this illness that unsettled her. They did all they could to tend to Minnie, with both Ada and her Papa staying up in the barn all night with her, trying to encourage her to eat a little food. But there was nothing to be done. Minnie died the following day, and Ada went behind the barn for a moment to cry for inability to save her.

That should have been the end of it. But the next day, Ada heard another pained moan from the barn, and another cow was soon gone. Then another cow fell sick, and another. Then the sheep, and the goats. Ada and her father worked tirelessly, barely sleeping, barely leaving the barn, only eating when Betsy or her family brought food to them, but they could not stop the onward march of the disease. The sickness was like a plague, spreading indiscriminately and felling all of the animals it touched.

Ada was in the barn with some of the sick sheep a few days after Minnie died, trying to coax them into drinking a little water or eating some of the warm mash she had prepared, when she heard her father give a shout. Ada raced outside to find her father leaning against the wall of the barn, clutching his side and wincing in pain.

"Papa?"

He shook his head at her. "I'm all right, Ada," he said. "My stomach just disagreed with me a bit there."

"Papa," Ada said, putting a hand on his shoulder and peering into his eyes. "You don't look well." She pressed a hand to his forehead. "You're burning up, Papa!"

Her father shook his head again. "I'm all right," he said. "Head hurts a bit, and I am a bit warm, but it's nothing to worry about."

"You should rest, Papa," Ada said. "I'll take care of the animals today."

"Can't do that," her father said, sounding pained. "Too much to do."

"I can do it," Ada said, but her father ignored her, and, grimacing, continued his way to the barn.

Ada tried her best not to hover over him for the rest of the day, but she could not resist forcing a warm stew into his hands at supper and insisting that he leave everything in the house to her to deal with that night.

But the next morning, her Papa could not rise from his bed at all. Sweat clung to his brow, and his face was burning with fever. Ada ran and fetched the village doctor, but even the doctor was mystified. He brought leeches to help cleanse her father's blood, and then shrugged and said to simply hope it was a temporary strangeness brought on by the loss of so many animals and nothing more.

Ada's father did not get better. She cared for him every moment she could, dabbing the sweat from his brow and talking to him in a soft, calming voice as he faded in and out of dreams, but all her time spent with her father meant she could not care for the animals as much as she should, and even more fell sick and died. She eventually begged help from Frank and Betsy to care for her Papa while she desperately tried to keep the farm running and the animals alive. She slept very little, running from one duty to another and staying up most of the night just watching her father toss and turn, but the animals continued to die, and her Papa only got weaker and weaker.

Ada found herself with tears in her eyes every time she paused for a moment, waiting to fill a bucket with water or dabbing her father's forehead with a cloth. She felt exhausted and overwhelmed, and none of what was happening felt entirely real, like it was all just a terrible dream she would soon wake from.

All that was left were the chickens then, and Ada wanted to sob when she thought of all that she and her Papa had lost. How would they feed themselves or earn money with all of their livestock gone? A few eggs a day would not be enough to sustain them. They could not even sell the fallen beasts for meat, because who would want to eat an animal that had died of such a curious illness that had also seemed to infect its master? Some unscrupulous butcher might be willing to buy it for a discount, but what if the sickness then passed on to his customers? Ada could not risk that happening for the sake of a few coins. She had grown up to be quite an expert with numbers and figures, but even she could not make money appear out of nothing, and the useless doctor was costing them what little savings they had. Even if her father recovered, they would not have the money to replace what they had lost.

But her father had to recover. She only needed to hold on, and things would be all right. Once he was better, he would know what to do.

Her father continued to fade, and one day, a couple of weeks after he first fell ill, he woke from his dozing and struggled to sit up.

"Don't strain yourself, Papa," Ada said. "The doctor said you need as much rest as you can get."

"I need to talk to you, Ada," he said. "Help me up."

Reluctantly, she helped him into a sitting position, supporting his back with the pillow.

"I'm not going to get better, Ada," he said, his voice hoarse.

Tears stung Ada's eyes, but she shook her head. "You will, Papa," she whispered. "Just you wait and see. You will."

Her Papa reached forward and grabbed her hand, squeezing it tightly. "I won't, Ada," he said. "That doctor's taken all our money, and he has no more idea of what's happening than I do. Less, in fact, cos he can't feel what I can feel. I'll be dead soon, Ada."

"No," Ada said, shaking her head fiercely, even though in her heart she knew what he was saying was true. "I won't let that happen."

"I don't think whether you'll allow it or not allow it will have much to do with it, my darling," he said. "So listen. I spoke to Frank yesterday, while you were out with the chickens. He's offered to take you to London with him and Betsy. They're due to leave next week, and I want you with them."

"I can't leave you," Ada said.

"You have to," her Papa said. "I'm leaving myself soon enough. If you go with them, you'll be able to get a job at that fancy London house too, and make a life for yourself."

Ada shook her head. "What about our farm?" she whispered.

"What farm?" he asked. "I know you've been trying to keep it from me, my dear, but I know the truth of what's happening. What's a farm without any animals? Just some buildings and some fields."

"I'll rebuild it," Ada said. "We'll replace the animals."

"How?" her father asked. "Don't pretend to me that that doctor was cheap."

She squeezed his hand fiercely, tears rolling down her cheeks. "We still have chickens," she said.

"Can't support a farm with only chickens," her father said. "Sell the chickens, Ada. Go to London and leave me here."

"I can't," she whispered. Her father broke into a fit of coughs.

"You must," he said, once he could speak again. "I won't think of you here alone, Ada. I couldn't bear it. You go to

London and live a great life. I love you, and I will miss you for all the time I have left, but this will be the best for you."

"But who will take care of you?" Ada asked.

Her Papa smiled weakly. "I'm not entirely without friends," he said, "after living my whole life here. I'll be all right. All I care about is taking care of you."

Ada wanted to argue more, but she saw the determination in her father's eyes. He usually looked vague and unfocussed since falling ill, but there was no uncertainty in his expression now.

"All right, Papa," she said, squeezing his hand and leaning forward to kiss him on the cheek. "I'll go, if that's what you want for me."

He nodded, and sank back down into the bed, his eyes drifting shut. As soon as he got her agreement, all the fight and energy seemed to fade from him. "Good girl," he said softly. "You'll be a good girl, I know you will. And I'll see your Mama soon."

CHAPTER 2

The week until Ada's departure passed much as the weeks before it had. Ada desperately hoped for a miracle, that one morning her father would have new strength in him again, but he continued to fade. He had barely spoken since she agreed to go to London. Ada arranged to sell the chickens, but every moment she secretly hoped that she would not have to leave after all.

Yet the morning came, and her father was barely coherent. Betsy's mother offered to keep an eye on him, but when Frank pulled the wagon to the front of the farm, ready for departure, Ada's father did not seem capable of even noticing a change in his companion. Ada kissed him on both cheeks, and then once on the forehead, tears streaming from her eyes. She took his hand and squeezed it, and then kissed it too, but her father made no response that suggested he even recognised her.

"I love you, Papa," she whispered to him. He moved his lips, but he did not form any words in response, and eventually Ada was forced to release his hand and leave the room. She looked back at her father one last time, from the doorway, and then wiped her eyes, picked up her bag, and walked from the house.

She climbed into the wagon beside Betsy, and Betsy wrapped her arms around her sobbing friend as Frank told the horses to walk on. Ada stared at the farmhouse where she had spent her entire life so far, her eyes fixed on her father's bedroom window, until they reached a turn in the road and it vanished from sight.

Ada spent most of that first day crying, her heart feeling as though it had been split in two. Betsy continued to hold her, crying with her for her best friend's pain and for the loss of a father figure that she had known since she was an infant too. They were a very sombre party when they settled down in an inn for the night, Betsy and Ada curled up tight in a bed together, and although Ada felt certain that she would never sleep for grief, the weeks of sleeplessness and a long day battered by the roughness of the road had exhausted her, and she soon passed out into a deep sleep.

By the following morning, Ada had cried herself out over her father, but she still spoke little, thinking constantly of what her Papa was doing, whether he was being cared for, and whether he was still with them on this earth at all. As the days passed, Betsy tried to cheer up her friend with tales of all the exciting things they would do in London, but Ada found it difficult to listen or to care. What did it matter what grand buildings or fancy people they saw, if her Papa was gone? Even if her wildest fantasies came true, and she met the rich London gentleman of her dreams, she would never be able to return home to the farm, and what did she care for a handsome husband, when she had neither her Papa nor her animals in the world beside her?

They travelled for nearly two weeks, and Ada settled into a resigned kind of grief. She did not speak much, but she listened to Betsy and her father talk, and she was grateful that the tiring nature of life on the road meant she was able to fall asleep almost as soon as she and Betsy lay down every night. She found it hard to feel excited or intrigued about the big city that was to be their destination, but she reminded herself that Betsy's father was doing her a great favour by bringing her along when she might have been left with nothing, and she felt grateful to him and to her friend for all her efforts to comfort her.

When their wagon finally reached the capital, Ada was so shocked by the sights and the smells that she temporarily forgot her grief. The streets were packed with horses and carts, and the floor of the wagon shook as horse-drawn cabs clattered past them at an incredible pace. Crowds of people walked on either side of the road too, and many strode across the road without any care, forcing Betsy's father to pull the horses up suddenly or risk trampling them. The air was thick with smog and smoke, and the *smell*. Ada was used to the smell of manure, but she had never smelt so much of it all at once before. The streets seemed covered with it. And when the cart came to a bridge over a great river, Ada and Betsy both gagged at the horrific stench rising from the water. Ada pressed her sleeve over her nose, and Betsy's father laughed.

"It's quite something, isn't it?" he said. "Not like home."

"What *is* that?" Betsy gasped.

"They got fancy sewers in the city," Frank said, "or the rich people do, and it all flows down into the river to be carried away. I wouldn't recommend you try for a swim in it."

Betsy turned green at the thought.

"It used to be different," Frank continued. "When I was a lad, big fish swam up that river. Sometimes you might even see a whale, if you were lucky. Of course, the streets stunk worse then, since that's where everyone's waste ended up. And the rain usually washed it into the river anyway, so you still wouldn't want to go for a swim. Don't worry, though. The rich folk have even more sensitive noses than the two of you, so they keep away from the stench. As for the rest, you'll get used to it."

"Is your friend *very* rich?" Ada asked. Frank looked at her, startled. She had barely spoken in days.

"I would say so," Frank said. "He's in trade, something to do with India, I believe. It's been twenty years since I last saw him, but I know he keeps a great house in one of the nicer parts of the city. He always promised he'd take on Betsy when she came of age. My father did a favour for his father once, and Mr Morter is the honourable sort. Never leaves a debt unpaid."

"What was his name again?" Ada asked,

"Edward Morter," he said.

Ada thought over the name. You could tell little from a name alone, but she hoped the man was kind. Surely he must be if he was keeping a promise made decades ago because of deeds done by their fathers? It was incredibly generous. Surely even the grandest of houses did not simply have space for anyone who might come along looking for work.

Ada's situation hit her suddenly, and she gasped. "But he's only expecting Betsy!" she said. Her grief had been so heavy for these past weeks that she had barely thought about their destination, but now realisation pierced through the blackness. There might not even be a place for her. "What if I'm not welcome?"

"Don't worry, Ada," Betsy said, putting an arm around her. "They'll love you, I'm sure."

But once Ada had thought about it, she could not put the worry from her mind. What would she do in this great city alone, if Betsy's father's acquaintance rejected her? She had no friends, and very little money. Would Betsy's father be willing to drive her all the way home again when he returned? Though there was little respite in that plan either. Her father was gone, and the farm along with him. She had nowhere to go.

"Stop fretting," Betsy said, more firmly this time. "It'll work out, you'll see."

But Ada had little faith in the idea of things working out well anymore.

They stayed with another of Frank's family friends for the night, and Ada did not sleep a wink. She lay perfectly still, not wanting to disturb her friend sleeping on the mattress beside her, and stared at the window, unsure whether she was desperate for the dawn or wishing that it would never come. She could not deny that being in London was exciting. Everything was loud and different and new, and despite the crowds and the stench, she felt buoyed by all the newness and opportunity here. But she was also terrified of what the morning would bring, whether she would settle into a secure future with her best friend, or whether she would be turned out onto the street with nowhere else to go.

She squeezed her eyes closed, and desperately wished she could talk to her Papa. More than anything else, she wanted his steady, soothing voice and his understanding eyes to reassure her that everything would be all right. But Papa was dead, and she had to take care of herself now.

Ada could barely eat the porridge that they were offered for breakfast, and even Betsy seemed to have trouble, her excitement overtaken by nerves. Seeing the tension on both girls' faces, and perhaps considering how it would look to pull up to a fine manor in a country wagon, Betsy's father suggested that they walk to the Morter House and take in some of the sights of the city. The streets were crowded with people again, but the crowd slowly began to thin out as the buildings on either side of the road grew fancier, turning from inns and warehouses to large town houses and finally to expansive manors with grass and walls around them, just like in the country. Ada still found the air oppressive, thick with smog and smoke, but the stench was more bearable here, and Ada found herself peering around at the buildings excitedly, taking in every elaborate detail.

"Ah, here we are now," Frank said eventually, and he nodded towards the end of the street, where the largest house Ada had ever seen stood behind a pair of iron gates.

"That's someone's *house?*" Betsy asked, in awe.

"It's about to be your house," her father said, laughing.

They approached the front gate and began to walk through, but Ada found herself stopping just before it, gaping at the size and grandeur of the house that awaited her. Surely she could never belong in place like this, not even as a servant.

"Watch out!" a man shouted from behind her, just before someone collided into the back of her. She stumbled as vegetables rained down onto the pavement around her.

"I'm sorry, miss," the man said hurriedly. "Are you all right there?"

"Yes," Ada said quickly. "Yes, I'm sorry, I shouldn't have stopped so suddenly." Unable to look at the man from embarrassment, she knelt down and began picking up as many vegetables as she could. They had fallen from an open sack in the man's arms, and he knelt too and began to put them back. She handed them to him without looking at him.

"It's all right," the man said. "It's a big house. I know I gaped when I first saw it."

"Do you live here?" Ada asked, risking a glance through her eyelashes at the man's face. He was young, maybe a couple of years older than her, with brown hair and soft brown eyes, and he was smiling kindly at her.

"In a manner of speaking," he said. "My name's Thomas Canton. I'm the cook here at Morter Manor."

"Oh," Ada said. She could feel her cheeks burning red. "My name's Ada. I mean-

Adeline. It's Adeline, but everyone calls me Ada. Ada Thompson."

"Well, it's a pleasure to meet you, Adeline known as Ada."

Thomas Canton stood and held out a hand to help her up too. She took it, still too embarrassed to fully look at him.

By this time, Frank and Betsy had noticed that Ada was not following them and had circled back to the gate. "You all right there, Ada?" Frank asked her.

She nodded. "I got in the way of Mr Canton here," she said. That was how you addressed strangers in the city, wasn't it? By their surname? "I'm sorry to be a bother."

"No bother at all," the man said. "You don't have to call me Mr Canton. It's just Thomas. Can I help you with anything, sir? What brings you to the Manor?"

"We're here to see the master of the house," Frank said. "Mr Edward Morter. He offered a job for my daughter Betsy, and I hope for her friend Ada here too, once they came of age."

"Mr Edward Morter, sir?" Thomas asked. He frowned, and then realisation seemed to hit. "I am sorry, sir, but the old master died a month back now. It is his son, Mr Philip Morter, who is in charge here now."

"Oh," Frank said. He looked taken aback. "I am sorry to hear that." Meanwhile, Betsy shot Ada a panicked expression, and Ada understood. Edward Morter had promised a position for Betsy, but there was no guarantee that his son would feel bound by those words. But although Ada felt panic for her friend, she felt a little less afraid for herself. She and Betsy were in almost the same position now, and although Betsy would be heart-broken if she were turned away, at least they would not be separated.

"Don't worry," Thomas said, seeing the look on Betsy's face. "The new master's a kind man. I'm sure there won't be a problem. Why don't I show you inside?"

"That would be very kind of you," Frank said, and Thomas hoisted the bag of vegetables higher in his arms and led the way around the back of the house into the kitchen.

Ada had never seen a kitchen like it. It was a large room,

with a huge metal range cooker against one wall and many pots and pans hanging from the walls. A line of bells hung just above the staircase. Three people were working in the kitchen already, two small girls scrubbing the floor while an older woman kneaded dough on the counter.

Thomas deposited the bag of vegetables on the side table, and with a nod to the older woman, he led the group up the narrow stairs and into the house proper. "What name is it?" he asked casually, as the climbed the steps.

"Franklin Johnson," Frank said, and Thomas nodded.

Ada had no experience with rich people's houses, but to her eyes, no grander home could possibly exist, unless you considered the houses of actual princes and queens. The floorboards were a deep rich wood, while the walls were covered in coloured paper decorated with intricate weaving flowers and vines. The ceiling of the hallway was high, high above them, and a rich patterned rug swept the length of the corridor, muffling their footsteps.

Thomas rapped on a door to the left, and then poked his head through the gap. "Sir," he said. "You have visitors to see you. A Mr Franklin Johnson, and his two daughters. He says he had an arrangement with your father."

"Ah, yes," a deep but surprisingly young-sounding voice replied. "See them in, please, Thomas."

"Yes, sir." Thomas stepped aside and gestured for the group to approach the door. He gave Ada a part nod, part bow as she passed and grinned at her encouragingly, before heading back for the kitchen stairs.

Ada lingered in the doorway as Frank and Betsy entered the room, rather wishing she could disappear. The room beyond set her heart racing more than anything else she had seen in London so far. The walls were not walls, but shelves, floor to ceiling, and every single one was filled with leather-bound books. Ada had never seen so many books in one place all at once. She hadn't even thought there were so many different books in the entire world, and for a moment she wondered if the master of the house had simply bought the same book over and over again, to fill the shelves, but a second glance told her that was not true. The books were different sizes, their bindings different colours, with different words written on their spines.

She could never have imagined this.

The room contained three plush armchairs, all arranged around an unlit fireplace. The mantelpiece was made of shining white marble, with a collection of strange objects atop it, including a brass clock in the centre and tall white vases decorated with blue designs. Another rug covered the floor before the fireplace, and there was a round oak table supporting a couple more books, some papers, and a single cup of tea.

Ada was so enraptured by the room itself that she almost missed the man sitting inside it. This, she supposed, was the master of the house, the Philip Morter that Thomas had mentioned. She had been right to think he sounded young. He looked little older than her and Betsy, maybe in his mid-twenties at most, with sweeping blond hair and sharp blue eyes. He was dressed in fine mourning clothes, with a black waistcoat and a silk cravat around his neck. He stood when the group entered, and his smile was warm and welcoming.

"Mr Johnson!" he said, as though he and Frank were old friends. "How great to see you." He strode forward and shook Frank's hand firmly. "You were a friend of my father, I believe."

"Yes, sir," Frank said. "Though I hadn't seen him for many a year. I am sorry to hear of your loss. The news did not reach us out in the country."

"It was a sad business," Mr Morter said. "The world is poorer for his passing."

"My apologies," Frank said, "for intruding on you. Your father and I had an arrangement, but I was not aware of his passing."

"It is no matter," Mr Morter said, smiling kindly. "My father mentioned you to me on multiple occasions. Your father did a great kindness to this family, and I certainly intend to honour that by honouring my father's offer." He looked over at Betsy and Ada. "However, I must confess I am surprised, he did not mention that you had *two* daughters."

"Ah," Frank said. "This is my daughter, Betsy, and her friend, Adeline Thompson. Ada has suffered a loss recently, and it was our hope that there might be room for both girls in the household."

Mr Morter looked at Ada, and his eyes sparkled with warmth. "The more the merrier," he said. "There's room for all at Morter Manor."

"Thank you very much, sir," Frank said, as relief rushed over Ada. She would not be sent home. She could stay with Betsy. She could feel a smile breaking across her face, but she did not think that was very servant-like, so she ducked her head and bobbed into a grateful curtsey.

Mr Morter glanced at the clock on the mantelpiece. "My apologies for seeming rude," he said, "but I have a meeting I simply must rush off to. Ask for Mrs Flax. She is the head maid of the household, and she will sort you out." He stuck his hand out to Frank again. "It was a pleasure to meet you, sir."

The group took the cue to leave, and when they stepped into the hallway, a kind-faced, rather round woman was already waiting for them there. "Ah, Mrs Flax," Mr Morter said. "I assume Thomas sent for you. Excellent. These girls will be joining your staff starting today. I trust you will get everything arranged."

"I will, sir," Mrs Flax said, and she smiled at the pair. With a nod of gratitude, Mr Morter strode away.

"Well, girls," Frank said. "This is where I leave you."

Betsy darted forward and threw her arms around her father. "Please come visit," she said.

"I will," he said. "And you'll have to visit me too, when you get the time." He squeezed her tightly, and then turned to Ada. "Take care of each other, you hear? And be good. Listen to Mrs Flax's instructions. I know you'll both make me proud."

And with that, Betsy's father departed too, leaving the girls alone with Mrs Flax.

CHAPTER 3

Mrs Flax took them upstairs and showed them to a spare room in the servants' attic. There was only one bed between them, and a narrow window overlooking the roof, but although Ada knew she would miss the open air of the farmyard, she was relieved they would be staying close. Now Betsy's father had gone, Ada was beginning to feel the ache of the loss of her father again, her awe at the house turning back into loneliness and fear. Betsy smiled encouragingly at her as they changed into the maid's uniforms that Mrs Flax provided, and Ada smiled back.

Once they had changed, Mrs Flax gave them a tour of the house, chatting about the master as she went. "I've known Master Philip since the day he was born," Mrs Flax said, "and you've never met a sweeter lad. Well, he has his flaws and his problems, like we all do. He could throw a fit over a lost toy or an unwelcome bedtime with the best of them, but you could always tell he had a good heart. The loss of his father has hit him hard, although he tries his best not to show it. He's the sort who wouldn't want his grief to burden anyone else, and we're all fairly heartbroken by the master's passing. But Master Philip is a good master so far, strange as it is to see him a man grown when I saw him in swaddling clothes."

Ada felt more and more at ease as she listened to Mrs Flax talk. There was something about her countenance that suggested she would not suffer fools, and Ada did not think she was a woman she wanted to cross, but she was kind and welcoming too. Ada was relieved. Mrs Flax did not have to welcome them so warmly, when they had pretty much been dumped on her unawares.

"We get up at five," Mrs Flax said, "because the master is always up at six, and we need to have all the fires burning in winter and the windows open and airing out the house in summer by the time he does. I'll give you fairly straightforward duties to start with, and if there's anything you don't know how to do, *ask*. I'd rather have someone show you than have you do it wrong and need to do it over again, or worse, you damage something that belongs to the family. It can be hard work sometimes, I won't deny it, but we are all something of a family here, and as long as you apply yourselves and listen to what you're told, you'll do very well, I think."

She led them down to the kitchen again. "This is where we gather when we're not working," she said, "and where you'll be doing most of your work too while we get you accustomed to the place." As she spoke, the back door opened, and Thomas strode in again. Flour was smudged on his face, and Ada could not resist smiling. "I hear you've met Thomas already," Mrs Flax said, and Ada and Betsy both nodded.

"Be careful with this one," he said to Mrs Flax, with a joking smile, nodding towards Ada. "She's a troublemaker. Knocked all my vegetables out of my arms on the way in."

"Oh, and I'm certain that wasn't your fault, Thomas Canton. You've never dropped something or made a mess in your life," Mrs Flax joked back. "Boy, you've got flour on your face at this very moment. Who are you going to blame for that one?'

"Just myself," he said, grinning, as he rubbed his face with his hand. He only succeeded in spreading the flour more around his face, and Mrs Flax gave a huff of disapproval.

"He's lucky he's so talented," Mrs Flax said. "Thomas here is the youngest cook I've ever known of, and he deserves it, too. I've never tasted such fine food, not in all my fifty years. And the *bread* he makes. It will be worth working here just for that, you mark my words it will."

Thomas's ears turned red. "She's exaggerating," he said to Ada and Betsy. "She always likes to tease me."

"Psh!" Mrs Flax said. "If you won't take a compliment, then go on with you and finish whatever it is you're meant to be doing. The girls will taste your cooking and see you for a liar soon enough."

"You wound me, Mrs Flax," Thomas said, pressing a hand to his heart. He smiled at Ada and Betsy again, gave them a respectful nod, and left the room again. Ada stared after him. He was a strange boy, she thought, handsome and apparently good-hearted, and she fancied he would be good company, once they got to know him.

"You're making eyes at him," Betsy whispered to her, giggling.

"I am not!" Ada protested, and Mrs Flax frowned.

"Now, we'll have none of that," she said. "I won't have any sort of impropriety in my household."

Ada blushed red. "No, Mrs Flax," she said. "Of course not."

Mrs Flax nodded, looking satisfied. "He is a handsome lad, mind, so be careful, the both of you. I've no doubt he's a heartbreaker, but we all have too much work to do to be fussing with that. Now, listen here, and I'll show you how the range works."

Over the next several days, Betsy and Ada met the rest of the servants and settled into life at Morter Manor. Ada was accustomed to hard work, after a lifetime on the farm, but this was labour of a rather different sort, and she found herself exhausted by the end of every day. But she appreciated the busyness, and the tiredness that swept over her as soon as she lay down in bed beside Betsy at night. As long as she kept busy, she could not think too much about the loss of her father, or the animals, or the home that she missed very much. She did not speak much to anybody, letting Betsy do the talking for them, but every time Thomas saw her, he offered a friendly comment or a joke, and Ada warmed to him bit by bit.

It was difficult to get accustomed to the riches in the house around her, and whenever Ada polished the silver or swept the fireplaces in the bedrooms, she found herself wanting to pause and just marvel at the finery on display. Nonetheless she resisted the urge. Mrs Flax was a kind-hearted woman, but she ran a tight ship too, and Ada did not want to incur her wrath in her very first week.

Several days later, when Mrs Flax sent Ada to light an evening's fire in Mr Morter's study, Ada could not stop herself repeatedly glancing at the bookshelves as she worked.

"It's Ada, isn't it?" Mr Morter said from his armchair.

"Yes, sir," Ada said.

"How are you finding things here, Ada?" he asked her.

"Very good, sir, thank you," she said. She could feel herself blushing, and forced herself to focus on the fire.

Mr Morter fell quiet, returning to his work, and when Ada rose to leave, she allowed herself to sneak another peek at the bookshelves.

"Do you like books, Ada?" Mr Morter asked, and Ada jumped. She had thought he was no longer watching.

Still, Ada would not lie. "Yes, sir," she said softly. "Or at least, as much as I can be. We never had access to many back home on the farm."

"What was your favourite?" Mr Morter asked her. "Of the books you did manage to read?"

Ada considered the question for a moment. Part of her felt compelled to give the *right* answer, whatever that might be, but what would be the point in lying? "I read a book by Miss Austen once," she said. "I liked that very much."

"Well, then," Mr Morter said. "You have excellent taste."

Ada bobbed a curtsey at him perplexed, and hurried from the room.

A FEW DAYS LATER, Ada found herself in the study with Mr Morter again. "You said you grew up on a farm, Ada," he said conversationally, as she worked. "What brought you all the way to London?"

Ada swallowed, steeling herself for the truth. "My Papa passed away, sir," she said. "Not too long ago. He wished me to come here and make a new life. We lost our animals too, so… there was nothing to stay for."

"I am sorry to hear that, Ada," Mr Morter said, and she was surprised by the sincerity of emotion in his voice. "It is always difficult to lose a father. I think perhaps I understand a little of how you feel."

Ada nodded and tried to continue focussing on dusting. But she could not stop her mind from whirring over his words, and she said, "Were you very close to your father, sir?"

"Not very," Mr Morter said softly. "I lived elsewhere until very recently. Although I find that I miss knowing he was alive in the world, even if I rarely saw him."

"His spirit is still here," Ada said, "or I believe so. We can't see them, but they watch out for us." She blushed furiously as she realised what she had said. "I'm sorry, sir," she said. "I shouldn't be so forward."

"No, you should," Mr Morter said. "You are very wise. I have had no one to talk to about this grief. I appreciate it."

Ada nodded. She did not know what else to say. She heard Mr Morter stand behind her and cross the room. He pulled a book off a shelf to her left and handed it to her. "Another by Miss Austen," he said, as Ada took it. "I hope you will enjoy it."

"Oh no, sir, I couldn't—" Ada said, but he shook his head and pressed the book firmly into her hand.

"You can and you should," he said. "The books are meant to be read. I insist."

AFTER THAT, Ada found herself frequently working in the room that Mr Morter happened to be in, and when she asked Mrs Flax about it, Mrs Flax admitted that Mr Morter had requested her. "He says you do a good job, Ada," she said, and then she frowned. "Why? Has he done anything inappropriate?"

"No, Mrs Flax," Ada said quickly. "Nothing like that. He lent me a book."

"Well, he always was a generous boy," Mrs Flax said. "It stands to reason he'd be a generous man too."

With Mrs Flax's approval, Ada began to feel a little less nervous about Mr Morter's kindness. He was a good man that was all. While she worked, he asked her how she was finding the book, so she told him, and they discussed the story together, and then another, and another. Sometimes he discussed his father, or asked Ada about herself. Other times, they worked in companionable silence, each leaving the other to their thoughts.

"Good day, Mr Morter," Ada said to him one afternoon, about five weeks after she started at the Manor, and Mr Morter shook his head, smiling.

"Call me Philip, Ada, please," he said. "Mr Morter was my father."

Ada was about to protest that that would not be appropriate, but she remembered Mrs Flax's approval of their friendship, and had to admit that of course the master of the house had the right to decide what he wished to be called. "All right," she said. "Philip." She felt an illicit little thrill as she said his name aloud, and the smile he gave her upon hearing his name was enough to brighten the entire room.

Lying in bed that night, Ada could not prevent her thoughts from wandering to Mr Morter — to *Philip* — as they had for many nights past. Thinking about him gave her butterflies in her stomach, and she could not stop herself from envisioning him kissing her sweetly one day. In her fantasy, he called her the sweetest, loveliest girl he had ever met, and begged her to forget the difference in their station and marry him. The Ada in her imagination of course accepted.

She buried deeper into the blankets, smiling to herself. It was a ridiculous thought, of course, but it was fun to imagine, just for a moment at least.

Life was good at Morter Manor. The spectre of Ada's father's death haunted her, and sometimes she felt so weighed down with grief that simply walking seemed like an impossible task, but she had Betsy beside her, at least, and the other servants were all kind too. They were a lively bunch, often joking alongside their work, and they made Ada smile despite herself almost every day.

The chief joker was Thomas. He never crossed a line that would irritate Mrs Flax, and he never slacked on his work, but he was always ready with a comment and a smile, his hair mussed from running his fingers through it in thought and flour almost inevitably on his face. But Mrs Flax had not lied about his abilities. Every meal that Thomas cooked was delicious, and his pastries were nothing short of divine. Once Thomas noticed Ada's soft spot for the treats, he started squirrelling some away from each batch just for her, and the two of them ate them together by the back step, when Mrs Flax was distracted, chatting and joking away.

"You didn't!" Ada gasped during one such conversation, as Thomas regaled her with tales of the pranks from his youth.

"I did!" he insisted. "I replaced all the salt for sugar. I'm surprised my Ma didn't hear me snickering in the corner while she cooked and figure it out."

"But it's so expensive!" Ada said.

"Well, I know that, and you know that, and my Ma *certainly* knew that, but little five year old Thomas most definitely did not know that. I did by the end of it, though! My Ma was so furious. I reckon I'm lucky to be alive here today."

"Psh," Ada said, giving him a little nudge with her elbow. "I'm sure she barely touched you."

"She didn't," Thomas said. "But listen to this. My punishment was to help with all the cooking and baking, so I could properly appreciate all the hard work I'd ruined. Well, the joke was on Ma, wasn't it, because turns out I loved it, and I've never stopped since."

"So you're saying that you're only sitting here today because you were a terrible menace as a child, and you've never stopped following your Mama's punishment since?"

"It's true!" Thomas said. "And my Ma, she took one bite of my first loaf of bread, and she said, 'Thomas, you can pull any prank you like, as long as you bake this every day.'"

"Okay, now that I *don't* believe," Ada said. "You are a liar, Thomas Canton."

"You're a smart one, Ada Thompson. The first loaf I made was pretty much inedible. It was more of a punishment for my Ma than it was for me."

"I never knew my Mama," Ada said quietly. "She died when I was a baby, and my Papa never spoke about her."

"Never?" Thomas asked.

"Sometimes I would ask him about her," Ada said, "but he would get so sad that it felt cruel to force him to remember. But now he's gone, I wish I'd asked more. I wish I had someone who could tell me about her."

"Well," Thomas said slowly, carefully, "the way I see it, you're your mother's daughter, aren't you? Part of her spirit is in you, guiding you. Some of your sense of humour is her sense of humour. Some of your talents came from her. So I think, if you look at yourself, and listen to your feelings, you know her better than you think."

Ada smiled. "That was really sweet, Thomas," she said. "Thank you."

Thomas shrugged. "Just seems true to me," he said.

"So did your Ma teach you all your recipes?" Ada asked.

"At first," Thomas said. "But, as you might have guessed, I wasn't always the best at listening to Ma's directions and following the rules."

"Really?" Ada asked, faking shock. "Never!"

Thomas chuckled. "So I started experimenting. And not salt-for-sugar stuff. Real experiments."

"How did it go?" Ada asked.

"*Terribly*. I didn't know the first thing about cooking, did I? I was just tossing things in and taking things out at random. My Ma got so frustrated with me wasting ingredients that one day she came home and she tossed this battered printed cookbook down in front of me. *Mrs Beadle's Handy Home Guide for Mothers and Wives*, it was called, but my Ma had crossed the last part out on the cover and replaced it with 'for Thomas'. My Ma said that if I was going to refuse to follow her recipes, maybe I could try those, or at least learn more about the rules so I didn't try to make bread without flour again."

"My Papa used to bring me books home too," Ada said. "Even

though we couldn't afford them, really. He brought me whatever he could."

"Well, that wasn't my last cookbook," Thomas said, "but it was my favourite. I still have it with me here."

"You do?" Ada asked, sitting up straighter in excitement. "Can I see it?"

"Hang on a moment," Thomas said. He stood up and peered through the ajar kitchen door, checking that Mrs Flax was still elsewhere. Once he was certain the coast was clear, he slipped through the door, and returned a few moments later holding a thick cardboard-backed book with ragged corners and many pages falling loose. He handed it to Ada like it was a great prize, and she took it carefully. Across the front, she saw the cheaply printed words, and his mother's handwritten addition.

She opened the volume with some reverence, and gasped as she found page after page covered with tiny handwriting.

"Was this all you?" she asked him, and Thomas nodded.

"I made a few improvements," he said, "over the years."

"And a few *un*improvements?" Ada asked.

"A few of those as well," he said, with a grin. "But only when the result was particularly entertaining."

Papa would have liked Thomas, Ada often thought. He was kindness personified, but light hearted too, always ready to invoke a smile, and Ada felt comfortable and free whenever he was around.

Betsy often teased her about their friendship, and Ada blushed and smiled and played along. She wondered what Betsy would say if she learned about Ada's friendship with Philip, but Ada did not mention it to her. It was not a friendship anyway, not really, she told herself. The master was just being welcoming and kind.

The first evening that Philip offered Ada a seat in his study to talk after she had lit the fire, Ada curtsied and refused him. She knew in her heart that Mrs Flax would not condone such behaviour. But Philip insisted, commenting on how tired she looked and how much he enjoyed their conversations while she worked, and he sounded so earnest that Ada could not deny him. Their conversations were already one of the highlights of her day, and it was soothing to talk about the loss of their fathers together when the melancholy struck them, and to discuss books and stories when it did not. Philip asked Ada many questions about her life on the farm, and he seemed delighted by her tales of frolicking lambs and disagreeable hens.

"I think I should like to live on a farm," Philip said, smiling. "Do good honest work with nature all around me, and see the fruits of my labour there."

"There's nothing better," Ada said, and then she blushed. "I mean—"

"I know what you mean, Ada," Philip said. "And I believe you're right. The city has nothing to offer in comparison."

That night, Ada found herself returning to her long-forgotten fantasy of being swept off her feet by a rich man in London and then moving back to the farm together to live out the rest of their days. It had been the ridiculous imaginings of a child, something unlikely to be found even in the most unrealistic of novels, but she could not resist returning to it now, with Philip taking the place of her handsome suitor. He paid attention to her every day, and he never said or did anything inappropriate. He simply seemed to appreciate her as a companion as a friend, and as their acquaintance grew, Ada began to think that perhaps, *perhaps*, the idea of him caring for her in such a way was not so impossible after all.

Then, just as Ada was settling into her life at Morter Manor, Philip's wife arrived.

CHAPTER 4

Ada was polishing the candlesticks in the hallway when the front door opened and a tall, thin young woman stepped inside. She looked to be in her early twenties, and she was more striking than beautiful, with a long nose and discerning brown eyes. Her hair was pinned elaborately on top of her head, and she was dressed almost uncomfortably fashionable, with a corseted waist and huge flowing skirts. Several rings decorated her fingers, and she wore a sparkling necklace around her neck.

She strode into the house like she owned the place, and Ada hesitated in her cleaning, clueless as to whom the woman might be.

"May I help you, ma'am?" she asked.

The strange woman looked down her nose at Ada, taking in all the details of her appearance. "Yes," she said. "I have bags outside with the carriage driver. Someone will need to fetch them and have them brought to my rooms."

"You're staying here, ma'am?" Ada asked. She had talked to Philip only the previous night, and Mrs Flax earlier that morning, and neither had mentioned the arrival of a visitor.

"I live here, you useless girl," the woman said.

It seemed rude to argue that the woman did not live there, because Ada had never seen her before in her life, so Ada just curtsied. "Let me fetch Mrs Flax," she said.

"Well, do it quickly," the woman said, as Ada scurried off.

Mrs Flax was working in the kitchen, but she looked up as soon as Ada descended the stairs. "Finished already, Ada?" she asked.

"No, Mrs Flax," Ada said. "A woman has come to the house. I've never seen her before, but she says she lives here."

"Oh dear," Mrs Flax said. "A tall woman? Young? Somewhat severe looking?" Ada nodded, and Mrs Flax sighed. "Of course she wouldn't think to write ahead and inform us of her arrival. She'll be furious we don't have a room prepared, but how are we to know, if she doesn't inform us? Dear me." Mrs Flax bustled off upstairs, and Ada, curious, followed her.

"Mrs Morter!" Mrs Flax said, as she stepped into the corridor. "What a wonderful surprise." Ada frowned. This woman could not be Philip's mother. She was far too young. Had his father remarried before his death, to someone about his son's age? Philip had never mentioned a young stepmother before, but if he were embarrassed by it, perhaps that was natural.

"Really, the help here gets worse every time I come home," Mrs Morter said. "No one has fetched my bags from the cab yet, and I've been here five minutes at least."

"I'll ask Thomas to do it," Ada said quickly, and turned back for the stairs.

"We weren't expecting you, Mrs Morter," Mrs Flax said.

"I told Philip I was coming," she sniffed, "but when can that man be trusted to think of anyone other than himself?"

"I'm sure it wasn't deliberate, ma'am," Mrs Flax said. "Perhaps the letter got lost."

"My husband does not need you defending him, Mrs Flax," Mrs Morter said, and Ada froze in the doorway.

"You're right, of course, ma'am," Mrs Flax said.

Ada looked back at the pair. She could not stop herself from speaking. "You're married to Mr Morter?" she asked. "Mr Philip Morter?"

"There is no other Mr Morter at this address," Mrs Morter snapped. She looked at Ada like she was an utter fool. "I am still waiting for my bags, girl!"

Ada bobbed her a rushed curtsey and scurried down the stairs, her heart pounding wildly. It couldn't be true. Philip was not married. She would know if he was. Someone would have mentioned his having a wife. Philip himself would have said something.

"Ada," Thomas said, when she entered the kitchen. "What's going on?"

"There's a woman here," Ada said. "She claims to be married to the master."

"Oh no," Thomas said. "There goes all our peace and quiet then."

"You mean it's true?" Ada asked. "The master is married?"

"Oh, he's married all right," Thomas said. "And to the worst sort of woman. Let's hope she doesn't stay long. She thinks being mistress of the house means nit-picking everything, and that was *before* the old master died."

"Ada!" Mrs Flax shouted, and Ada jumped.

"Right," she said. "She wanted you to carry in her bags from the cab."

Thomas rolled his eyes, but nodded and strode out of the back door of the kitchen, leaving Ada to hurry back upstairs after Mrs Flax.

The next couple of hours were dizzy with activity, as they prepared Mrs Morter's rooms for her use and provided an unexpected luncheon for the mistress. Ada did not dare ask any more about the woman while the work was being done, but she awaited Philip's return to the house later that afternoon with anxious trepidation. How would he react to the sudden appearance of the wife he had never mentioned?

The confrontation between Philip and his wife, if it could truly be called that, occurred in the hallway, almost as soon as Philip had hung up his hat and coat. Ada was working in the study with the door ajar when she heard the front door open and close, and Mrs Morter swept out of the sitting room towards her husband.

"Felicity," he said. "What a surprise."

Ada could not help herself. She crept to the open door and peered through the gap. Mr Morter was looking at his wife with a thin smile on his face. Ada could not see his wife's expression.

"It shouldn't be a surprise," Felicity Morter said, "since I wrote to you repeatedly. You told me you would be returning to Bath."

"That was my intention," Philip said, "but matters required extra attention here."

"Yet you did not invite me to join you."

"My dear, I know you value Bath society far greater than you value mine. I assumed you were happy there."

"I would be happier," she said, "if my husband paid me any attention whatsoever."

"If you wished for a husband who loved you," Philip said, "you should not have insisted on marrying me."

Ada gasped. If she had not seen and heard it all herself, she was not sure she would have believed it. Philip had always been unceasingly kind and polite to her and everyone else she had ever seen him speaking to. She would not have imagined that he could say such harsh words to his wife.

But then, she had not imagined that he *had* a wife. She was beginning to wonder if the Philip she had thought she knew really existed at all.

His wife sniffed in response. "You really must see about the servants," she said. "They are terribly incompetent. Wherever did you find that new girl? *Ada*"

"On a farm," Philip said, and Ada flinched back, stung. He had never spoken so dismissively of her before. "Now, if you will excuse me, my dear." And Philip strode up the stairs and out of sight.

It wasn't until the servants' dinner in the kitchen that night that Ada was able to find out more about the situation.

"It won't do to talk ill of the mistress," Mrs Flax said, "but then, she's been no true mistress of mine. Cold and vindictive, she is. Luckily for the master, she never stays in one place for too long. She has too many friends for that."

"So you think she'll be leaving again soon?" Betsy asked.

"Well, before this, she was the master's daughter-in-law," Mrs Flax said. "Now she's the mistress of the house. She told me she plans to remain for a while yet, so the master will not be pleased."

"I never knew he was married," Ada said quietly.

"The master doesn't like to talk of her," Mrs Flax said. "We're all forbidden from mentioning her when she's not here, she irks him so much."

"Why did he marry her," Ada asked, "if he dislikes her so much?"

"His father wished it," Mrs Flax said. "He thought it would be a good match for the family. But now, see how miserable his son is. Just goes to show what good meddling in young people's affairs will do."

But Ada's heart was not satisfied. It was foolish, she thought, to have ever imagined that Philip might have any intentions towards her, but it felt dishonest that he had never even mentioned his wife. To be married but to act the bachelor... it did not speak well of him at all.

"You all right, Ada?" Thomas asked her, once the meal was finished. "You look bothered."

"I'm just surprised Mr Morter is married," she said. "To not ever mention it, and to forbid everyone else from mentioning it too…."

Thomas gave her a look that was a little more sympathetic and understanding than Ada would have liked. "He's a strange one, for certain," he said, with gentle lightness. "I wouldn't worry about it, Ada."

But Felicity Morter's presence proved impossible to ignore. She had brought her own woman with her, so none of the regular maids needed to care for her fire or help her get dressed in the morning, but that did not prevent her from harassing them as they worked in the rest of the house. As soon as she had finished her breakfast the following morning, she ordered Mrs Flax to bring Ada and Betsy into her presence, and she looked them both up and down with narrowed eyes as they stood before her and waited for her to speak.

"Your father is a parasite on this family," she eventually said to Betsy. "You realise that, don't you?" Betsy paled, but she said nothing. "You are not suitable to be a maid. You belong in the mud of the country, not in a grand house like this. Because of this *agreement*, we're forced to accept you and pretend you might be of any use at all. And *you*." She turned her gaze onto Ada. "*You* are worse. There was no arrangement for a second daughter."

"No, ma'am," Ada said. "But Mr Morter was kind enough to take me on anyway."

"From a *farm*," Felicity sniffed. "How novel." She scowled. "As mistress of the house," she said, "it is my duty and my right to choose the staff. I did not expect to return from an absence to find that two little country rats have been hired without my consultation."

Ada bit her lip. Suddenly, she imagined this woman throwing her and Betsy out on the streets. Betsy's father had long since left the city, and they had no other friends here, and nowhere else to go.

"Please let us stay," Betsy said desperately. "We're not trouble. We do good work, Mrs Flax says we do. We won't be a bother."

"Your presence is a bother," Felicity said. "But my *husband*," she emphasised the word with great disdain, "has overruled me. He insists you remain. I cannot imagine why. Well," she added, narrowing her eyes. "I *can* imagine, but you had both better hope no such behaviour is occurring in my house, or you will be very sorry."

Betsy blushed and looked down, but Ada felt indignant. "What are you implying, ma'am?" she asked.

"I am implying," Felicity said, "that your relationship with my husband is not proper, and that he did not truly hire you for the role of a maid. Do I need to speak plainer?"

"You are mistaken, ma'am," Ada said. Her voice shook slightly. "It is not like that."

"I am glad to hear it," Felicity said. "Make certain it remains that way. Now get out of my sight."

Ada and Betsy hurried away, both of them blushing furiously. "I can't believe she would think— well, *that*," Betsy whispered to Ada, as they headed to the stairs down to the kitchen. "Like Mr Morter would ever take notice of us like that. Like we would *want* him to."

Ada nodded vaguely in agreement, but inside, she was in turmoil. She felt like all her foolish thoughts had been ripped bare and revealed for the wickedness that they were.

But she had not known, she insisted to herself. She had not known he was married. She had never truly expected him to pay attention to her. And they had never done anything inappropriate, not even in her own wildest imaginings. Her only crime was being a fool, thinking that Philip might have grown to care for her, when in truth he was married all along.

That evening, Philip requested that Ada once again come and bulk up the fire in the study, and Ada fought to keep her expression as neutral as she could manage it as she entered the room. He was sitting in his usual armchair, a book open on his lap, and Ada bobbed a respectful curtsey to him before hurrying over to the fireplace and kneeling before it.

"Ada," Philip said, with false cheer. "I missed you last night. But I found I had no time to myself as I would like."

"Of course, sir," Ada said softly, without looking at him. "You must have been eager to spend time with Mrs Morter."

He snorted. "Not quite," he said.

"As you say, sir."

He started to rise, and then seemed to think better of it, and sat down again. "Ada," he said. "I—"

She paused, but he seemed at a loss of what to say next. What excuse or apology could he possibly make? Felicity Morter would exist no matter what he said.

She stood up and turned to the door, still not looking at him. "Have a good evening, sir," she said, and she scurried from the room before he could reply.

The frustration and embarrassment drove Ada to work twice as hard, and that was lucky, because Felicity was a strict mistress, and soon everyone was running about desperately trying to keep up with her demands. Her standards were exacting, her mood always sour, to the point that she even found fault with Thomas's wonderful cooking. Every day, Ada grew to resent her a little bit more, and even Mrs Flax could be heard muttering about her unreasonableness, prefacing each complaint with a comment that "she shouldn't speak ill of the mistress" before ploughing ahead with it anyway.

Ada avoided Philip as much as she could. Any work that might bring her into his proximity was handed off to someone else in the house, and if she truly could not escape it, she did her duties as efficiently as possible, offering only the barest comments to him that politeness required.

Philip did not push the issue. He seemed to have difficulty looking at Ada sometimes, and Ada thought it might perhaps be guilt over his grave omission. She found that she missed their talks, but she knew that was just her foolishness influencing her again. Their talks had never meant anything. She was just a maid, and she should not forget it.

CHAPTER 5

"Ada!" Felicity shouted, one rainy autumn day. "Ada, get here at once!"

Ada had been dusting in the empty study, but she hurried to the entrance hall once she heard the shout. Hesitating would only make whatever was about to happen worse.

Felicity stood in the entrance hall, surrounded by a shocking mess. Muddy footprints covered the wooden floorboards, and water pooled by the door.

"Yes, ma'am?" Ada asked, bobbing into a curtsey.

"It's like a sty in here," Felicity said. "How could you have let it get so dirty?"

Ada had done nothing of the sort, but it wouldn't help her to argue. She knew that Felicity had just said goodbye to a party of ladies taking tea in her sitting room, and the mess could only be the result of many delicate boots and hemlines dragging through the dampness on their way from the cab to the front door of the house. But it would not help to mention that either.

"I'm sorry, ma'am," Ada said.

"Just because *you're* used to living in filth," Felicity said, "that doesn't mean the rest of us are. Clean this up at once!"

"I don't live in filth," Ada said quietly. "I never lived in filth." It was dangerous to argue back, but Felicity's words stung more than Ada would have cared to admit. It was one thing for Felicity to insult Ada; she did so daily. But to insult her old life, her precious memories on the farm with her father and the animals... that she could not bear.

"You lived with the pigs and the sheep," Felicity said, "and now you bring those habits here. You should never have become a maid."

"We never kept pigs, ma'am," Ada said. "And they're very clean animals. My home was never anything so filthy as London."

Nobody who had been to the countryside could have denied that. The filth of London seeped into everything. The smell was not particularly bad around Morter Manor, but the dirt in the air coated the windows if left undisturbed for too long, and the pollution sank into the wallpaper, discolouring it slowly.

"Do not speak back to me," Felicity said, "you ungrateful wretch."

"What happened in your meeting, ma'am," Ada asked, "that has upset you so much?"

Felicity strode forwards, and Ada felt certain she was about to slap her. Then a voice shouted from the top of the stairs. "Felicity! What on earth are you doing?"

Philip strode down the stairs.

"Directing the maid," Felicity said haughtily, "as is my job. Look at what she has allowed to happen to the hallway!"

"I am certain your guests and the rain had nothing to do with it?" Philip said mildly. "It is all on poor Ada's head."

"Mind how you speak about the maids, Philip," Felicity said, eyes gleaming with malice. "Or one might make assumptions."

"Of course, my dear," Philip said. "I am going to my study. I suggest you find something else to occupy yourself as well, so that the maid can actually begin the work you're so insistent on."

He walked to his study without another word, and Felicity watched him leave, eyes narrowed. Once he was gone, she spun back to Ada. "You heard him," she said. "Clean! Now! If this place is not spotless within the hour, I will make you very, very sorry."

She strode away, her heels clicking as she went, and Ada headed down to the kitchen to fill a bucket and fetch a mop. Thomas was lingering by the doorway at the bottom of the stairs, listening.

"She's a nightmare," he said, when Ada appeared, grimacing sympathetically.

"It's fine," Ada said. "It's my job."

"Even so." Thomas went to collect the bucket for her and walked to the tap to fill it.

"You don't have to do that," Ada said, but Thomas just shrugged and smiled.

"I want to," he said.

"I can lift it!" Ada insisted, as he began to carry the full bucket to the stairs.

"I know you can," Thomas said. "You're stronger than I am. But I still want to help."

He not only carried the bucket upstairs for her, but grabbed a cloth himself and began to scrub the floor. Ada got down beside him, scrubbing too.

"This way," Thomas said cheerfully, "you'll get it done twice as fast."

"This can't be how you want to spend your time," Ada said softly, as she worked.

"Of course it is," he said with a grin. "I get to spend it with you."

"You are such a flatterer, Thomas Canton," Ada said, but she could not hide her smile.

"Is it flattery if it's the truth?" he asked, and she laughed.

"You must have given your mother so much trouble," she said. "You can't be argued with. You always have an answer for everything!"

"Trouble?" Thomas asked. "I'm positively charming."

"See?" Ada said. "How did she put up with you?"

Thomas continued laughing to himself as they worked. "I've no idea," he said. "She would like you, you know," he added.

"What's she like?" Ada asked.

"Fierce," he said. "Like you. And kind. Also like you."

Ada felt herself blushing. "Maybe one day I'll be able to meet her," she said.

"Yes," Thomas said quietly, almost to himself. "I hope you will."

They cleaned in silence for a few minutes more, each lost in their own thoughts. "What was your father like?" Thomas asked eventually. "If you don't mind speaking of him."

"No," Ada said. "I don't speak of him enough." She paused and looked at the wooden floor for a moment, thinking. How could she capture her Papa in words? "He was generous," she said. "And kind hearted. He was so gentle with all the animals. It was as though he could speak their language. He always understood what they needed, and the animals always trusted him to help them."

"I've never been around animals much," Thomas said. "I mean, there are the barns in the city, and you see cows being herded down the street every now and again, but I've never gotten close to one. Never spoken to one."

"Do you imagine a cow would be a good conversationalist?" she asked with a smile.

"I imagine they would be good listeners," Thomas said. "And I'd like to try to understand them."

"They do have eyes that look like they understand you," Ada

said. "Even if you don't say a word out loud to them, they look at you like they know what's in your heart."

"Do you miss it?" Thomas asked softly. "The animals, and the farm?"

"Yes," she said. "Every day. I never meant to leave. I wanted to spend my entire life there. It was my home. Those animals were my home. But after the sickness came, there was nothing left. Without my father, and without any animals… what reason was there to stay?"

"Maybe you can return one day," Thomas said. "Rebuild."

"I would like that," Ada said.

"And I'd like to see it," Thomas said. "When you do."

"Bring your Ma," Ada suggested, and out of the corner of her eye, she saw Thomas smile.

"I think I will."

WITH THE TWO of them working together, the hallway barely seemed to take any time to clean at all, and when Felicity returned an hour later, she could not say anything in criticism of Ada despite her sneer. Ada changed into a clean uniform and went to help in the kitchen, and the evening had long drawn in when Mrs Flax approached her and told her she had been summoned.

"Mr Morter wants more wood on the fire in the study," she said. "He asked for you specifically." She narrowed her eyes suspiciously at Ada, and Ada found herself blushing. Why would he summon her now? Did he not realise it would only get her into more trouble with Felicity? He had seemed happy to forget the connection they'd forged since she returned. And now he wished to see her.

"Of course, Mrs Flax," Ada said. "I'll go at once."

She hurried to the study, and then paused outside the door,

smoothing out the wrinkles in her skirt and composing herself. She managed to open the door calmly and bob into a curtsey without really looking at him, before heading over to the crackling fire.

"Ada," Philip said. "Please look at me."

She could not ignore the entreaty in his voice. She looked up. He sat in an armchair with a book balanced open on his lap. His hair was mussed as though he had run his hands through it many times, and beside him she could see a half-empty whisky bottle and a crystal glass.

"It's been so long since we've talked, Ada."

"We've both been busy, sir," Ada said.

"Call me Philip, Ada," he said. "I've told you before."

"As you say, sir," she said.

Philip looked frustrated. He dug his fingers into the hair at his scalp again, messing it up further. "Come sit, won't you?" he said. "The fire is fine as it is."

"Then why did you ask me to rebuild it, sir?"

"Philip!" he shouted, and Ada jumped. "Call me Philip!"

Ada's heart began to race. She just looked at his frustrated face, uncertain what to do. She had never seen him act this way before.

"I wanted to apologise," he said, "for the way Felicity treats you and your friend. I want to apologise for Felicity in *general*. Believe me, Ada, if I had had a choice, I would not have married her."

"I was under the impression that rich men can direct their own lives," Ada said.

He laughed bitterly. "Not when my father wanted her family's business connections. And see what good that has done us. He is dead, now, and I'm alive, stuck with her." He refocussed his eyes on her. "Sit, Ada!" he snapped.

Ada did as he asked. Her hands shook slightly on her lap, and she pressed them against the arms of the chair to stop them.

"I'm sorry," Philip said, running his hand through his hair again and sighing. "I should not have shouted. Please forgive me. I am very tired."

"It's all right," Ada said softly.

"It is difficult to be one's best self," he said, "when your wife despises you."

"She can't despise you," Ada said, but he shook his head.

"It is true," he said. "She wants me to be more than I am. She wanted a business genius, someone aristocratic that she can show off at parties. She resents me for who I am. But perhaps that is fair. I am not fond of her character either." Ada did not know what to say, so she said nothing, and Philip took another sip of his drink and continued. "She is jealous of you," he said, "because she knows I do not despise you, like I do her. That is my fault." He shook his head. "I am sorry," he said, "that I did not tell you about Felicity. It was unforgivable of me."

"It is no matter," Ada said carefully. "You don't have to explain yourself to me. I'm only a maid."

"Not to me," Philip said passionately. "Never to me, Ada." He stood up suddenly, and Ada jumped. He marched forward and seized her hands, dropping to his knees before her. "You must know how I feel about you, Ada," he said. "How I've felt ever since I first saw you. I *love* you, Ada."

Ada gaped at him. Part of her heart sang with joy to hear his words, but her mind knew better than to believe it. He was married. Nothing could ever come of any feelings, even if they did exist.

"You have been drinking, Philip," she said softly. "You don't know what you say."

"I *do* know," he said. "I have wished to say it for weeks now. It kills me to see you avoiding me. You are beautiful, Ada. Beautiful, and witty, and kind. You *see* me, Ada. Felicity has never seen me."

Ada tried to slide her hand free from his, but he would not let go.

"I need you, Ada," he said. "I *need* you. Tell me you need me too."

"You're married, Philip," she whispered.

"I'm married for business," he said. "My heart is free. Or it was, until I met you. Now it is yours. I want you beside me."

"Philip, what—"

"Be my mistress," Philip said. "I will treat you so well. You would not need to be a maid any more. I could send Felicity away, and you could live here with me, or we could both leave together. I will buy you the silks and jewels that you deserve to wear, and we will travel, Ada. We will see the places in your books. Paris, if you like. Farther. Rome, perhaps."

Ada gaped at him. "I cannot," she said eventually.

"We can travel," Philip insisted, "and I will tell everyone that you are my wife, if you prefer it. I will give you everything you deserve."

"You cannot," Ada whispered, "because you are married, and I deserve to be a true wife, not a mistress."

"What are words and titles?" Philip said. "What are they compared to emotion, to love?"

"It would be improper," Ada said, her heart racing. "Please do not ask this of me."

"And why shouldn't I?" he asked. "Why must I give up all happiness in my life, because of *her*, when you are right here, and we go so well together?"

"Please," Ada said, pulling her hand away and standing. "I cannot do this, Philip. Please do not blame me."

He stared up at her, his expression dark, and for a moment, Ada thought he was going to shout at her, maybe even strike her. Fury burned in his eyes. Then he blinked and stood.

"Go, then," he said. "I do not require further help this evening."

"Yes, sir," Ada said. She bobbed a curtsey at him and fled from the room.

∼

ONCE SHE WAS SAFELY BACK in the hallway, Ada leaned against the wall, her legs barely able to support her own weight. Her heart pounded against her ribcage.

She had not been wrong. In fact, even her craziest thoughts had not gone far enough. Philip claimed to *love* her. But it was only a claim, wasn't it? He was drunk. If he truly loved her, he would not insult her in this way, asking her to dishonour herself and betray all her honour and dignity on his behalf. Would he?

When Ada felt certain she could walk again, she raced up the stairs to the room that she shared with Betsy. Betsy was already there, sitting on a little stool by the window and brushing her hair before bed. Her eyes widened when she saw Ada's expression.

"What is it, Ada?" she asked. "What's happened?"

Ada told her, as clearly as she could. Betsy gaped at her as she spoke, her eyes growing wider and wider with every word.

"He asked you to be his *mistress*?" she repeated finally.

Ada nodded.

"I can't believe it," Betsy said. "And you turned him *down*?"

Ada blinked at her in surprise. "Of course I turned him down," she said. "It wouldn't be right."

"Who cares about that?" Betsy asked. "You would be rich! He offered you jewels, and *travel*. You could go anywhere in the world. You wouldn't have to live in the attic and work for your supper anymore."

"I would," Ada said softly. "In a different way. I would be beholden to him. I wouldn't be free."

"We'll never be free," Betsy said. "At least this way, you'd be treasured. And *rich*. Who is offered an opportunity like that and turns it down?"

"Are you saying you would have *accepted* him?" Ada asked.

Betsy shrugged. "He hasn't given me the opportunity, has he?" she said. "Although if he turned to me now, after your rejection, I'm not certain I would say no. That life would be better than this one."

"It wouldn't be right," Ada said. "He's *married*."

"To a wretch of a woman he despises," Betsy said. "That just makes the situation even more sense."

Ada sank onto the bed, unable to believe what she was hearing. "I thought you would agree with me," she said.

Betsy shrugged. "Well, I don't," she said.

"I'm scared, Betsy," Ada said. "What if he throws me out for rejecting him? I have nowhere else to go."

"He said he loved you," Betsy said waspishly. "If that's true, he won't turn you out onto the street."

"But he seemed so angry," Ada said.

"Then perhaps," Betsy said, "you shouldn't have refused him."

Ada felt tears burning in her eyes, and she fiercely wiped them away. Had she truly done wrong? If *Betsy* was condemning her...

Ada's heart would not permit her to regret her decision. Anything else would have been a sin. She *knew* it was wrong.

Yet even so, she could not stop herself from curling up into a ball in the bed beside Betsy and silently crying herself to sleep.

CHAPTER 6

Ada barely slept that night. She tossed and turned in bed, her heart broken by Betsy's apparent rejection, terrified of what the morning would bring. When she rose and headed down to the kitchen the following morning, her eyes were bleary with exhaustion.

"What's wrong, Ada? Thomas asked, as he kneaded the morning's bread. "You look exhausted."

"It's nothing," she said, rubbing her eyes. "Just didn't sleep well."

"You sure?" Thomas asked. "Cos it looks like something was keeping you up."

"No," Ada said. "No, it's nothing." She could not bear anyone else dismissing her or calling her a fool, as Betsy had done. Besides, if news of Philip's proposition reached Mrs Flax, what would become of Ada then? Ada had rejected the master, but Mrs Flax had been clear that she would not accept any hint of impropriety in her household. Would she hold Ada accountable for Philip's words and actions if she knew?

To Ada's relief, Philip seemed as determined to avoid Ada as she was to avoid him, and she did not see more than a glimpse of him for days. Felicity continued to be harsh to her and Betsy, but it was no harsher than she had been before, leading Ada to believe that she did not know what had transpired in her husband's study.

Ada waited for the hammer of truth to fall, for Mrs Flax to summon her and tell her she was being asked to leave the house, but the moment did not come. Philip had told nobody of his proposition or of her rejection, and Ada began to hope that he would not take retribution against her after all.

She did, however, notice that Thomas watched her more often, and spoke to her less, than he had before. Frequently, he opened his mouth as though to speak to her, and then Mrs Flax or one of the other maids would enter the kitchen, and he would quickly close it again and say nothing. It was unsettling. All Ada could think was that Thomas suspected what had happened, and did not know how to bring it up. But Ada would prefer it if he *never* mentioned it, and so she began to avoid being alone with him, insisting that she was too busy to talk. She did not know how she would react if Thomas, of all people, mentioned Philip's proposition. She could only hope that he did not know anything definite, and that he did not think badly of her for what he did know, but there was little she could do to ensure either of those outcomes other than avoid him.

One day, about two weeks after Philip's proposition, after the servants had eaten their dinner in the kitchen together, Thomas approached Ada and asked if he might speak to her privately outside.

"Oh," she said, feeling herself blushing furiously. Betsy was watching her out of the corner of her eye. "I can't. I still have so much to do. The dishes—"

"You go on, dear," Mrs Flax said, smiling knowingly. "You've been working too hard."

Ada nodded, desperately trying to think of another excuse, but none would come, so she was forced to walk towards the kitchen door with Thomas. But just as they reached it, another maid appeared in the kitchen door, saying that the cook was being summoned by Mrs Morter at once.

Thomas pulled a rueful face at Ada and turned, and Ada smiled sympathetically at him, but she could not regret the interruption.

"Strange," Mrs Flax said, staring at the stairs after him when he had gone. "The mistress doesn't normally want to speak after the meal."

"Maybe there was something wrong with it?" Betsy asked, and Mrs Flax tsked.

"There's nothing wrong with anything we make here," she said. "Even the mistress must be able to see that."

But when Thomas returned to the kitchen, he looked pale. "What was that about?" Mrs Flax asked him, and Thomas shook his head, looking a little lost, and sank into a chair.

"She said the dinner made her unwell," he said. "She wanted to know what I put in it. She shouted at me for five minutes about using spoiled ingredients."

"Spoiled ingredients?" Mrs Flax repeated. "Now there's an insult. We would never do such a thing."

"That's what I told her, but she wouldn't listen. She was furious. Crying, almost. And she did look pale and sickly. When I suggested that perhaps she was unwell and needed to see a doctor, she threatened to have me kicked out and told me to get out of the room."

"What did the master say?" Mrs Flax asked.

"Not much," Thomas said. "I heard him suggest that she might need to lie down as I left."

"Dear me," Mrs Flax said. "The mistress is bad enough at the best of times. If she falls ill, then the Lord help us all. She will be unbearable."

The mistress was up most of the night, shivering and sweating and wracked with stomach pains. At one point, Mrs

Flax suggested they might run for the doctor, but Philip shook his head. "She has always had a sensitive constitution," he said. "Rest and time will settle whatever wrong thing she ate."

But neither rest nor time had any positive impact on her. By morning, she was feverish, rolling in the bedsheets, murmuring nonsense to herself. It was clear to everyone that this was no food complaint. They ran to fetch the master, and when Philip saw her, his expression turned grave. "Call the doctor," he said. "At once."

The doctor was sent for with all haste, and Philip sat by his wife's bedside and held her hand in silence as they waited. Ada's assistance and experience was also recruited, in attempting to make the mistress comfortable and coaxing her to drink a little to refresh herself, and the situation with Felicity was so dire that Ada hardly thought to feel awkward in Philip's presence. All past propositions became irrelevant when his wife lay so sick before them.

Ada certainly did not like Felicity, but she did not want her to die, and she knew that Philip must feel the same. It was one thing to wish a person gone from your life in a frustrated moment, and quite another to see them actually ailing and fading away.

The doctor arrived, but he could offer little. He diagnosed her with a fever, which they all already knew, and warned the household to keep a distance in case it was contagious. Philip refused that last piece of advice, remaining staunchly by his wife's side while the doctor administered leeches and gave her a little laudanum to calm her.

Ada remained in the room as well, at a greater distance, twisting her hands together in front of her from fright. The sight of the doctor with Felicity brought back too many memories of her father ailing in bed, the sickness that had suddenly overtaken him. Could something like that be happening here?

Had she carried the sickness to London somehow and spread it to a new house?

The doctor left, and Felicity did not recover. Philip stayed by her side for the rest of the day, squeezing her hand comfortingly, as her murmuring grew softer and the fight in her seemed to leech away.

"Philip," Ada said softly, after night had fallen. "You need to eat. You need to rest."

Philip shook his head, and Ada stepped closer. "She's asleep, Philip," Ada whispered. "Staying right now will not help her. It will only hurt you."

Philip considered his sleeping wife for a long moment, and then he nodded. "You are right, Ada," he said. "Of course. Will you watch her for me, while I rest my eyes? I will not be gone long."

"Of course," Ada said. "For however long you need."

Once Philip had departed from the room, Ada took his place in the chair by Felicity's bedside. A little sweat still clung to the woman's brow, but her expression was peaceful, and Ada gently smoothed the blankets over her and then sat back and looked across the room at the darkened window.

"Where is my husband?" Felicity murmured, her voice rough, and Ada jumped. She looked back at her charge to find her lying unmoved with her eyes closed.

"He has gone to rest," Ada said. "He will be back soon."

Felicity tried to laugh, but the sound broke down into a bitter, broken cough. "Of course," she murmured. "What else should I expect? Shirking his duty, even now."

"He has not left your side all day," Ada said. "I had to insist that he went to rest, for his own good."

"A maid should not be insisting on anything to her master," Felicity said.

"As you say, ma'am," Ada said, and Felicity laughed again.

"Bring me some water," she rasped, and Ada hurried to do as

she asked. She helped to prop Felicity up and brought the cup to her dry lips. Once she had drunk her fill, Ada placed the cup back on the bedside table.

"Would you like me to read to you?" she asked uncertainly.

"Is that what you do for my husband?" Felicity replied. "Do you *read* for him too?"

She did not seem to expect an actual reply, so Ada only sat again, leaving the book where it was beside her.

"What does my husband see in you?" Felicity asked. "You are not rich. You are not beautiful." She coughed again. "I never stood a chance, you know," she added, in a softer voice. "Our parents wished us to marry, and that was reason enough for Philip to despise me. As though my freedom was not being limited just as much as his. I had no choice, of course, no matter what he might believe. My father desired the match, and I would not fail or disappoint him. But Philip could never forgive me for that. I was so popular before I married him. I had so many suitors offering to dance with me at every ball. My dance card was never empty, and my chaperones quite despaired. But Philip does not like balls. He does not like dancing. He does not like company. Being married to him is like being already dead." She shook her head. "I do not know why I am telling you this," she said. "Dying makes me wish to speak, while I still can."

"You are not dying, ma'am," Ada said, but Felicity shook her head.

"Do you think I'm not clever enough to know when I'm dying?" Felicity said. "Do not insult me, girl, any more than you already have."

"Ma'am," Ada said slowly, "I want you to know that truly, nothing has happened between your husband and I. Truly it has not."

"But he has asked you," Felicity said. "I know he must have."

Ada could not lie, so she said nothing.

"He will not accept your refusal," Felicity said. "He is a man who very much likes getting his own way, and he is not used to be denied. Another count against me, I think, when we married. He did *not* wish to marry me, and his father made him anyway. What an insult my existence is to him. What a sign of weakness I am to him." Felicity sighed and closed her eyes. "He must have told you many stories," she said, "about how terrible I am. I know he forbids the servants from even mentioning me when I am not here. And I am usually not here, because who would want to be in a place where you are loathed and unwanted? In Bath, I am popular. In Bath, I have friends and engagements. Here, I am just a burden." She laughed. "I wish I were dying in Bath," she said. "I would have people who actually care for me beside me. Not a husband suddenly feeling too guilty to leave my side, and a maid who wishes to supplant me."

"Why did you come back, then?" Ada asked her. "Why have you stayed?"

"Why?" Felicity repeated. "Because this is supposed to be my home, and I am supposed to be mistress of it. People gossip if I never come back, and with my husband so recently bereaved... I have hated every moment being here, but be here I must."

"Did you ever care for Mr Morter?" Ada asked her.

Felicity raised her eyebrows at Ada. "You get more impertinent by the day," she said. But after a pause she continued. "Yes. Once. He is handsome and charming, is he not? Perhaps I did not love him, but I saw him when our families dined together, and I admired him. It was only after our parents pushed for our marriage that he turned cold." She turned her head, pressing her cheek against the pillow. "Go now," she said. "I wish to be alone."

"I promised the master I would watch you," Ada said.

"I do not need a maid to watch me die," Felicity snapped. "I want some peace. Now get out."

"Ma'am—"

"Out!" Felicity shouted, and Ada curtsied and fled.

Ada's conscience would not allow her to go far. She sat

down on the floor of the hallway, directly outside the door, out of Felicity's sight but still within hearing in case anything went wrong. She waited patiently for Philip to return, listening as Felicity fell into another restless sleep, tossing and turning and murmuring indistinctly. Ada fell asleep in the hallway, her head resting on her knees, and awoke several hours later to an eerie silence. The house was still dark, and not a soul seemed to stir

Ada got carefully to her feet and listened. She could no longer hear Felicity moving in bed or muttering or moaning. Perhaps she had finally found a peaceful sleep, she thought. She tiptoed back to the doorway and peered in.

Felicity lay still beneath the bedsheets, her head tilted to one side. She was not moving. Ada crept closer, holding her breath in fear, but Felicity's chest did not rise and fall.

"Ma'am?" Ada whispered.

Felicity had already gone.

CHAPTER 7

*A*n eerie silence settled over the house after Felicity's death. No one present had particularly cared for her in life, but her loss was still a terrible shock, and many a member of the household began to regret how they had thought of her now that she was gone. A young woman, with no health complaints to speak of, getting sick and dying in the space of forty-eight hours? It was a terrifying, unsettling thought.

The whole household dressed in black for mourning, and Mrs Flax was kept busy arranging for the funeral with Philip. Ada cried many tears for the mistress when she found a moment alone. She could not help but feel guilty for what had transpired. She had never wished Felicity ill, but she had disliked her presence, and her own behaviour had been presumptuous and inappropriate enough for Philip to feel comfortable asking her to be his mistress. Worse, her behaviour had been obvious enough that Felicity had been aware of all that transpired. She deeply regretted all that had occurred, and she could hardly imagine how guilty Philip must feel. She knew Philip had a good heart, and it must cause him agony to think that the wife he had been so cold to was gone, and that he had been resting elsewhere while she spent her final moments alone.

Part of her wished to comfort him, but that felt inappropriate too. She did not know how to conduct herself now. Betsy gave her suspicious glances whenever they worked side by side, as though waiting to see how Ada might respond to this new sequence of events, but mostly Ada just wished that the events of the past several weeks could be undone.

A couple of days after Felicity's funeral, Mrs Flax sent Ada to clean inside the study, and she entered to find Philip slumped in an armchair, close to the fire.

He glanced at her, and she curtsied, before he turned his eyes back to the flames, saying nothing.

She worked in silence for several minutes, forcing herself not to look at him, until he spoke.

"Ada," he said. His voice was raspy for lack of use, and even that one word sounded like it pained him to speak. "Please, stay a moment. Sit with me."

Ada hesitated. She knew that she should politely refuse, but he sounded so *broken*. If she was feeling guilty over what had occurred between them, he must be absolutely wracked with guilt and regret for insulting a woman who had then been taken from them so suddenly. Her heart ached for him, and nothing about her disposition would allow her to hear a man suffering so and leave him to face it alone.

She slowly crossed the room and sat in the armchair beside him. Philip looked at her now, and his eyes were red and shadowy.

"I am sorry, Ada," he said. "I am sorry for what I have done."

"It will be all right, Philip," Ada said softly.

But Philip shook his head. "I have behaved appallingly," he said. "Truly I have. How could I have asked you, a woman of so much purity and intelligence, to be my mistress? How could I have insulted you so?"

Ada was so startled that for a moment she could not speak. Surely he meant to say that he was sorry for his behaviour because of the insult to his now-deceased wife.

"You were not responsible for Felicity's death with your actions," Ada said. "They were misguided, perhaps, but she did not die because of you."

Philip shook his head again. "I should never have married her," he said. "I should never have given in to my father on this. We made one another miserable for all the time we were together. You lectured me, Ada, for saying that I did not have free choice, and you were right to. What sort of man am I, to harm myself and others so terribly, against my own better judgement, and then claim it was not truly me who had done it?"

"It is all right," Ada said. "It is over now."

"You are right," he said forcefully. "Of course you are right. It is over now. I have a new chance, to start again, to do things as I should. I was trapped, Ada, you understand, with Felicity as my wife. We would never have made one another happy, not for as long as we lived. I might have ruined my life with that mistake. But I have a new chance." He turned and seized Ada's hand with both of his. "My dear Ada," he said. "Dear, sweet Ada. I am sorry for the insult I have caused you. I can only beg you to forgive me, and to believe me when I say I see the truth now. I see the man I must be. Please, Ada, marry me. Be my wife, and make me happy again."

"Marry you?" Ada repeated. She could not have heard him correctly. "You wish me to be your wife?"

"Yes," Philip said. "More than anything, yes."

"I am a farmer's daughter," she said. "I— I am just a maid."

"You will not be, when you marry me. You will become a businessman's wife. I will give you all I promised you, Ada, and more besides, but with honour now. You cannot refuse me. You care for me too, I know that you do."

"I—"Ada shook her head. "Your wife has been dead not two

weeks. The entire household is in mourning. It would not be proper—"

"A period of a few weeks is respect enough," Philip said. "I have seen it before. No one will be shocked by us. And I cannot wait, Ada. I must have you beside me."

"Philip," she said. Her thoughts were racing. She had imagined such a proposal, in her silliest moments before she slept at night, but now that it had come, she felt no joy or excitement at the prospect. Instead, heavy dread had settled in the pit of her stomach. "I do not know what to say. This is so very sudden."

"I told you before of my feelings for you," Philip said. "You cannot be surprised by my proposal, now that my wife is gone."

"But I am, sir," she said. "I am. Please, give me a little time. I need time to think."

"Your heart does not tell you your answer immediately?"

"Please," Ada said again. "I hardly know what to say. Please give me a day or two to collect my thoughts, so that I may make you an eloquent and sincere reply."

"Very well," Philip said, releasing her hand. She stood up as soon as she was free, trembling. "A day. Two at most. I cannot wait any longer, Ada. I need you beside me."

Ada nodded. "By your leave," she said, and hurried from the room.

CHAPTER 8

Betsy waited outside the study door, her mouth agape. When Ada saw her, she pressed a finger to her lips to silence her and dragged her upstairs to their room.

"Ada!" she said, in a fierce whisper, once they were entirely alone. "He asked you to be his *wife*?"

"You were eavesdropping?" Ada asked.

"I was passing by," she said, "and I heard the master speaking so intently, I could not help but hesitate a moment. And then when I heard *your* voice, I knew that something important must be occurring. And I was right to, was I not? How can you be so foolish, Ada, hesitating and asking for time to consider? What if he changes his mind?"

"I'm not certain that I *want* to marry him," Ada said slowly. "It is so soon after his late wife's death. It seems wrong."

"Ada," Betsy said. "Girls like us do not receive offers to marry men like him. What is there to consider? Even if he was a terrible man, you would have more luxury and comfort than either of us could ever dream of otherwise. And he is *not* terrible. He is handsome and kind. He cares for you. What could there possibly be to think about?"

Thomas's face floated up in Ada's thoughts, unbidden. It was such a foolish and unexpected thought that for a moment Ada was left quite speechless. Thomas was a kind man, and she liked him very much, but he had shown no such interest in her. And besides, Betsy was right, wasn't she? Who would choose to marry a cook, when the master of the house himself had proposed to her?

"I just don't know if it's right," she said to Betsy. "His wife so recently dead, and me just a maid — perhaps he will regret it, Betsy. Perhaps this is just a fancy, and he will resent me like he resented his past wife soon enough. He is kind, Betsy, but he asked me to be his mistress. A man willing to do that once must surely be willing to do so again. He has regrets now, I know, and he mourns for his wife and the insult he did to her, but how do I know he truly is a changed man, and has not just been swayed by the emotion of the moment? It is a big decision, Betsy."

"You *must* do this, Ada," Betsy said. She grabbed Ada's hand and squeezed it. "You must. You will change all our fortunes if you do. Once you are mistress of this house, you will be able to elevate me from a maid to a true friend of the family. I am certain the master has many eligible young business associates that he might introduce me to. And then we could climb in society together, and travel and wear silks and be so much *more* than we ever could have dreamed of otherwise. Don't you see that? This is our chance. For *both* of us."

"But I do not know if Papa would wish it," Ada whispered.

"*I* know," Betsy replied. "Of course your Papa would wish it. Your Papa was a sensible man. He wanted you to be secure and loved and well-cared-for, didn't he? He wanted you to leave the farm and come to London to build a new life for yourself, once he could no longer care for you. This is an opportunity beyond his wildest imaginings, I am certain. He would insist that you accept him. I know that he would."

However, Ada knew that that last assertion, at least, was

untrue. If her Papa had met and liked Philip, he might have been pleased by such a proposal, but he would never have pressured Ada to marry him, not even if Philip were the king of England. He cared about Ada's happiness more than he cared about any man's rank or wealth.

Still, she squeezed her friend's hand before she let go. "I know, Betsy," she said. "It is just all so much. I am sure I will think as clearly on the matter as you do, once I have slept on it."

Betsy did not seem completely satisfied with this answer, but before she could reply, they heard Mrs Flax shouting up the stairs, demanding to know where her lazy maids had disappeared off to, and they were forced to end their conversation.

MRS FLAX CHIDED them once they returned downstairs, but not particularly harshly, and then sent Ada down to the kitchen, where, she said, Thomas was wishing to speak with her. Mrs Flax smiled somewhat knowingly as she said it, and Ada was confused over what he could possibly wish to say that was so important. She simply curtsied to Mrs Flax, however, and hurried down the stairs to meet him.

Thomas was chopping vegetables at the counter, but he stopped as soon as she emerged. "Ada," he said, and he rubbed his hands on his trousers rather nervously.

"Mrs Flax said you wanted to speak with me?"

"Yes," Thomas said. "I did. I do. I— I've been wanting to speak to you for a while, Ada, but so much has been happening... but Mrs Flax says if I hesitate for too long, I will lose either my chance or my nerve."

Ada had never seen Thomas look so uncertain. "Whatever is the matter, Thomas?"

"I love you," he said. Ada stared at him. "I've loved you ever since I met you, Ada, since I bumped into you outside the house and you helped me pick up all those vegetables. I know I don't have much, Ada. I have very little to offer you. I can only even propose to you in the kitchen of a house I could never hope to own. But I have a little money saved up, and I can promise I would take care of you, and love you as you should be loved."

"Thomas," Ada said. "Are you proposing to me?"

"Yes," Thomas said. "I'm sorry, I should have said that part. Yes. Please, Ada, will you marry me?"

"But I can't," she said, without thinking. "Philip just proposed to me too."

"Philip?" Thomas asked, frowning. "Mr Morter? He asked you to marry him?"

"Yes," Ada said, feeling utterly miserable. "Not half an hour ago in his study."

"My apologies," Thomas said, his back stiffing into a more formal stance. "I did not realise you were engaged."

"No," she said. "I'm not engaged. I don't know what I am. I told him I would have to think about it. I don't know what I want. I never thought— well."

Thomas nodded, looking at the floor. "You're considering it," he said, "but you'll accept him, won't you? How could a man like me compete with one like him?"

"That isn't it at all," Ada said desperately. "I don't know what I want, Thomas. I never thought Philip would propose to me. I never knew you had any such feelings for me at all."

"He is a rich man, though," Thomas said. "And our employer. It would be wise for you to accept him."

"Well, maybe I don't want to do what is wise," Ada said, tears stinging her eyes. "Maybe I want to do what my heart tells me to, and this is all so sudden that I don't know what that might be. Please, Thomas. I am sorry for ruining your proposal like this. I just need time to think. Just give me a little time."

"Of course," Thomas said, and he offered her a sad smile. "I am sorry for making you feel pressured. It would be a big choice to make, even without any other complications. Take as long as you need to think about it. I'll respect whatever choice you make."

"Thank you, Thomas," Ada said. She realised she was crying harder now, his kindness touching her heart. "Please don't hate me."

"I could never hate you, Ada," he said. "And I am sorry if I startled you."

She shook her head. "I do care for you, Thomas," she said. "I hope you know that. You have been such a good friend to me. The thought of never seeing you again would break my heart, truly it would. I just— I need time to think."

"Of course," he said. He lifted her hand to his lips and kissed it, like a gallant gentleman might to his lady. "Take all the time you need."

CHAPTER 9

Ada spent another nearly sleepless night tossing and turning while Betsy slept softly beside her. Her situation seemed impossible, and no matter how much she worried and obsessed over the events of the day, she could not think of a single way to resolve things without making it even worse. She imagined herself married to Philip, a mistress of a household with a fancy library of books and servants to help her and no concerns about food or money for the entire rest of her life, but the image no longer had the shine to it that it had had when she was an idly dreaming child. She kept picturing Thomas's heartbroken face, and a lifetime with him working in the kitchen, forever now beneath her, or worse, no longer in the house or her life at all.

When she tried to imagine being married to Philip, the image was softer, but still untenable. She could not be his wife and remain a maid in the household, serving the man she had rejected in favour of the cook. Thomas probably could not remain either. She imagined the two of them returning to her farm, buying new animals, living a life there like she had once dreamed, but then she thought of her father's death, and the anger that would undoubtedly fill Philip's face if she rejected him.

Perhaps Philip, she thought, would return to the farm with her. He had mentioned liking the idea of a farm life, before all of this occurred. But the idea of something and its reality were rather different things, and when Ada tried to imagine Philip at home on the farm, he was replaced by Thomas's face.

She could reject neither; she could accept neither. In which case, she thought, perhaps it was wisest to make the choice that would do the least harm, to herself and to others. The safest choice certainly seemed to be to accept Philip. Thomas would not blame her if she refused him. But Ada's father had always taught her to follow her heart, and was that what her heart truly wanted? She did not know.

When the dawn came, Ada dressed in silence and headed down to the kitchen. Half of her was afraid to see Thomas again, to see the hope on his face, but the other half of her yearned for his calming, sweet presence after a rough sleepless night. But when Ada reached the kitchen, Thomas was not there. Mrs Flax was cooking the breakfast, looking harried. She barely glanced up when Ada and Betsy arrived.

"Good," she said. "You're up. I need both of you. Betsy, grab that pan there. Ada, fetch me some eggs. Goodness, what a morning."

"Where's Thomas?" Ada asked. "Is he sick?"

"Thomas was fired by the master last night."

"What?" Ada and Betsy both gasped together.

"I know little more than you do," Mrs Flax said. "The master simply told me that I needed to tell Thomas to move on. He said he was no longer welcome here. Well, it's not my place to criticise the master, but it seemed cruel and sudden to me, so I tried to persuade him to reconsider, but he was insistent. In a fury, he was. I think he's blaming Thomas for the mistress's death, since she got so sick after that meal, in which case we're all lucky the master is not contacting the police. But I told him, Thomas had nothing to do with that illness. But what can we do?"

Betsy turned to look at Ada, her face white. But Ada was already running up the stairs, Mrs Flax shouting after her. She tore into Philip's study to find the master pacing in front of the bookshelves, his hands clasped behind his back.

"Philip," Ada said desperately. "Sir. I've just heard. Please don't kick Thomas out. He's a good man, Philip. I'm certain he can't have done anything bad."

"It's too late," Philip said coldly, and Ada flinched at his tone. "He's gone. If only you would show such concern for me."

"What do you mean?" Ada asked.

He whirled to face her. "I know about his proposal," he said. "I *know*, Ada. A kitchen boy, trying to compete with me. I couldn't allow him to remain and complicate matters."

"I—how?" Ada asked him.

"One of the maids overheard the two of you," he said. "Your friend, Betsy. She came straight to me."

"*Betsy?*" Ada cried. It couldn't be. *Betsy* had eavesdropped on her? Betsy had run to Philip to get Thomas kicked out of the house.

No, Ada realised. Betsy had turned white when she heard that Thomas was gone. She most certainly must have spoken to Philip, but she had not imagined things would go this far. Still, Ada felt the sting of the betrayal. She had known Betsy wanted the improvement in situation that would come for both of them with Ada's marriage to Philip, but to go behind her back and tell Philip her secrets, to interfere to ensure that Ada had no other choice... how could a lifelong friend do such a thing?

"Ada, you never mentioned, that you had another suitor in mind when you told me you needed time to consider."

"I didn't!" Ada said desperately. "I had no inkling of how Thomas felt about me. I meant what I said. Please, Philip.

Thomas needs this work. Where will he go? His entire life is here."

"That is not my concern," Philip said, "and it should not be yours either. Unless you are implying that you truly do prefer a kitchen boy over me?"

"He's not a kitchen boy," Ada said. "He's a cook, and he's a fantastic one."

"A cook?" Philip repeated. "Compared to *me*?"

"It's not a comparison!" Ada cried. "Truly, it is not. Please. I do not want him to be out on the streets for my sake."

"Then you accept my proposal?" Philip ask, and Ada flinched back at the intensity in his words.

"I don't know," she said again. "I need time. But please, stop this cruelty."

"You have *had* time," Philip said. "You had time, and you went running to this *boy* for distraction. You were too good to be my mistress, Ada, and yet you wish a chance to be with that fool?"

"*No*," Ada said. "It is not like that. Please."

"Enough!" Philip shouted, cutting her off. "Enough. I am not an unreasonable man, Ada. You will have until this evening to make your decision. Either you marry me, or you will be thrown out onto the streets to be with your precious kitchen boy."

"Philip, please—" Ada said, reaching for his arm, but he shrugged her away and strode to the door of the study. She heard the lock click behind him as he departed.

Ada ran to the door anyway and shook the door handle, willing it to open, but of course it would not. Then she ran to the windows, but these, too, were locked tight. She considered the ornaments on the mantelpiece, wondering if one of them might perhaps be strong enough to break the glass, but even if she succeeded in climbing outside the window, Philip's study was around the rear of the house, above the entrance to the kitchen, and at least twenty feet off the ground. She might well break her leg in the jump, and then she could run nowhere.

Ada closed her eyes, forcing herself to remain calm. There was no need to panic, and no need to flee. She knew now that she could not possibly marry Philip, not with his selfishness and temper and need to control her, but he had given her a choice, hadn't he? Become his wife or end up on the streets. When he returned, she would make her choice known, and leave through the door with dignity. He was angry with her, but he loved her, didn't he? He would not hurt her, not physically, if she refused him.

A voice inside her whispered that that was not true, that he had already fired Thomas and locked her away to decide, but what else could she do? She tried the door again several times that day, and the window too, but both were locked tight, and she passed the day pacing up and down in the study, forcing herself to keep breathing as calmly as she could.

The sun had set by the time Ada heard a key in the lock. The door was yanked open, and Philip stumbled into view, pulling it shut behind him.

She knew immediately that Philip was drunk. She could smell the alcohol on him from the other side of the room, and she instinctively flinched back when his eyes fell on her.

"Well?" he asked her. He stumbled forward, and Ada took a step back. "Have you reached your decision?"

"I have," Ada said. She was proud that her voice barely shook.

"And?" he prompted. "What is it to be?"

"I must decline your offer, sir," she said.

"Decline?" he repeated, his face turning red with anger.

"Yes, sir," Ada said. "After the way you have conducted yourself, I would rather be homeless and alone on the streets of a city I barely know than be your wife."

"How dare you?" Philip shouted. He stormed across the

room and seized Ada by the arms, and she cried out as his fingers dug into her flesh. "You dare speak to me that way? A little farm rat like you, refusing *me*?"

He shook her as he spoke, and she cried out again, fighting to escape from his grip. He held on tightly, so she kicked him in the shin, as hard as she could, and he released her, cursing. He stood between her and the door, so she stumbled backwards, grasping for a candlestick holder from the mantelpiece for a weapon.

"You *rat*," Philip said. "You do not get to refuse me. I killed my *wife* for you."

Ada froze. It was as though time stopped, all the air vanishing from the room. "You killed her?" she gasped.

"I offered you the position as my mistress," he said, "and you refused. Felicity was standing in our way, making us all miserable. She needed to be dealt with. Now we can have a fresh start, build our lives together. But you do not get to refuse me. Not after all I have done for us. Do you hear me, Ada?"

He started across the room towards her again, and Ada stepped away, her back colliding with the bookshelf. She hoisted the candlestick in her hand, ready to fight. If Philip had been willing to kill Felicity, he would have no qualms about murdering her. She would *not* accept him. She would not be tied to a murderer; she would not be ruled by fear. She would fight with every breath she had, and if she failed, at least she could pass from this world with the dignity of knowing that she had done all she could.

Philip grabbed her by the wrist, wrenching the candlestick from her grasp, and she cried out, struggling against him.

Then the door to the study crashed open, and Thomas barrelled into the room.

CHAPTER 10

"Ada!" Thomas cried. He dove for Philip as three policemen ran into the study behind him. Philip swung a punch at Thomas, but he stumbled from drink as he did, and Thomas dodged it, grabbing the other man by the arm.

The police soon seized Philip and yanked his hands behind his back into handcuffs, while Thomas hurried over to Ada and wrapped his arms around her. She pressed her face into the soft cotton of his shirt, trying to quell her sobs of terror and relief.

"It's all right, Ada," he said. "It's all right. You're safe now."

"How?" she asked, through her sobs. "How did you find me?"

"I will always find you," he said. "I will always be here for you. No matter what. I promise."

"But Philip—"

"Two weeks ago, Philip came to me and told me that his wife was insisting on a new, special ingredient to be added to her food, for health reasons. It was just a spice, so I didn't suspect much. It was only this morning that I realised it could have been a poison. I snuck back into the house to grab it and took it to the police as soon as I could."

"But Thomas," Ada said. "If you put it in the food, what if—"

"That was a risk," Thomas admitted. "But I'm safe now, thanks to you. The police overheard everything, Ada. We arrived just in time to hear his confession. He won't be able to blame me for it now."

"Oh, Thomas," Ada said, and she pulled him close and sobbed into his shirt again.

"It's all right, miss," a policeman said, as Philip was hauled out of the room, cursing up a storm as he went. "We'll just need to ask you a few questions."

Their questions were thankfully brief, and Thomas stayed beside her throughout, holding her hand and offering her silent support. Once the policemen were satisfied, they departed, and Mrs Flax burst into the room, her hair a mess, her face white with fear.

"Ada," she said. "My poor girl. My poor girl." She pulled Ada into a tight hug as well, and Ada hugged her back, tears pooling in her eyes as the relief overwhelmed her. "I am so sorry, Ada," she said. "I never thought—"

"None of us did, Mrs Flax," Ada said. "None of us except Thomas."

Betsy lingered in the doorway, looking as pale as a ghost, staring at Ada and Thomas.

"I'm sorry," Betsy said. "Ada, please forgive me. I only wanted... I never
thought—"

Ada rose to face her friend. "I forgive you," she said softly. "You did not know what Philip was like, or what would happen. But you betrayed me, Betsy. You went against me for your own greed. I forgive you, but I am not certain I will be able to forget."

"I'm so sorry, Ada," Thomas said. "If I had known the trouble it would cause, I would never have proposed to you. To think of the danger I put you in..."

"*Philip* put me in danger," Ada said. "And without you, and without Betsy, I suppose, I never would have known how truly dangerous he was, possibly not until it was too late. I am grateful, Thomas."

"I am still sorry I hurt you," Thomas said, but Ada shook her head.

"You didn't," she said. "You could never hurt me. Thomas," she began haltingly, uncertain how to express the feelings in her heart. "I am sorry too, for my reaction to your proposal. I was overwhelmed, and I was afraid too. I think I sensed that Philip would not allow me to refuse him, but as soon as I heard your offer, I knew where my heart truly lay. I knew, Thomas, but I was afraid, for myself and for you. And I'm sorry for it, I truly am."

"What are you saying, Ada?" Thomas asked her, hope clear on his face.

"I am saying that I would like to accept your proposal," Ada said. "If you will still have me."

"Yes!" Thomas said. "A thousand times yes!" He pulled her into another embrace, and she went into it gladly, before reaching up on her tiptoes and pressing a sweet kiss to his lips.

WITH PHILIP LOCKED AWAY for murder and no heir in place to take over Morter Manor, the household soon dissolved, but Ada was not sorry to see the last of the house. For a few weeks, Ada moved with Thomas into his childhood home, until everything else could be arranged. The first time she met Thomas's mother, the older woman pulled Ada into a tight hug and declared her the prettiest, sweetest thing she ever saw. Thomas's mother, it turned out, had also grown up on a farm before moving to the city, and she spent her evenings with her sewing on her lap, telling her son and soon-to-be daughter-in-law about her own misadventures and the manner of farming forty years before.

Soon, Thomas's mother was telling Ada to call her 'Ma,' and

Ada gladly accepted. Her new bond with Thomas's mother was bittersweet, as she desperately wished her father could have been there with them, that he could have met Thomas and given them his blessing, but with Thomas and his mother beside her, Ada felt safe and secure for the first time since her father fell ill.

Betsy found employment with another grand family, and Ada bid her a polite farewell, but she could not be too grieved that her friend would now be out of reach. Perhaps their relationship could mend with time, she thought, for Betsy had good intentions, and she had not realised what her actions would cause, but for now the fact remained that Betsy had betrayed Ada and hurt both her and Thomas deeply, even putting her life-long friend at risk of murder. It was difficult to know how to act around her, so an acquaintance built on occasional letter writing might be just the thing for them now.

Ada and Thomas had a small wedding at a chapel near Philip's childhood home, attended by Thomas's mother, Mrs Flax, and a few other servants from the old household. Afterwards, they all gathered in a nearby park, where they were met by several of Thomas's mother's friends for a small celebration. Thomas used a little of his savings to pay for new Sunday best clothes for himself and his bride, and Mrs Flax gathered flowers for Ada's bouquet and baked treats for the occasion.

After the wedding, Thomas and Ada began discussing their new long-term plans. It was Thomas who first suggested they return to Ada's family farm, using the rest of his savings to buy some more livestock, and Ada was so deliriously happy with the suggestion that she threw her arms around him and burst into tears, leaving her unable to give an actual reply for several minutes.

"What about you?" Ada asked, once she recollected herself. "What about your cooking?"

"I can cook there as well as here, can't I?" he said with a smile. "And I've been thinking. You take care of the animals, and

I can take the milk and the butter and the eggs and use them to bake our own farm treats. We can open a shop and sell most of what we make."

"All right," Ada said. "Under one condition."

"What's that?" Thomas asked.

"We ask your Ma if she wants to come with us. I'll miss her too much otherwise."

"So will I," Thomas said, grinning broadly. "Let's hope she says yes."

Ada returned home with her new husband and mother not one year after she and Betsy had departed. It was not precisely how she had imagined returning from the capital when she was a girl dreaming of romance, but, she thought, she rather liked it better. Thomas marvelled at the countryside, full of delights he had never dreamed of, gaping at the rolling fields and sighing in the fresh, unpolluted air. Thomas's small savings proved enough to purchase some new sheep and cows, along with a small flock of chickens for their eggs, and Ada set about teaching Thomas about the farming life. He stroked the sheep with a look of awe on his face, but he was more than a little nervous around the chickens, and would jump every time one clucked too loudly or pecked too close to his feet. Ada loved standing outside the coop watching him spread feed on the ground and eyeing the chickens like they might all turn on him and devour him, and although she could never quite bring herself to tease him about his nervousness, his mother had no such compunctions. She laughed heartily at her son's antics, declaring her mirth, her reward for the years spent bringing up such a mischievous troublemaking little boy, and once Thomas's mother started laughing, Ada could not help joining in too.

Thomas and his mother were quickly welcomed into the village. Although people could be a little strange about newcomers joining such a small community, Thomas was so friendly, and his treats were so delicious, that within a week everyone was acting as though they had known him for years, and within a month, their new little farm shop was the most popular place for miles around.

During the day, while Ada cared for the animals and Thomas baked, Thomas's mother sat in the shop, knitting away with her own home-grown wool, and gathering all the gossip from everyone who came by. Once evening fell and the animals were safe in their beds, Ada and Thomas would sit with Ma by the fire as she caught them up on everything she had learned, and every day, Ada's heart felt even fuller than it had the day before. The farm was alive again, and the warmth and laughter of her new family helped sooth away the shadows left by the sudden plague and the loss she had suffered.

She felt the absence of her father on the farm every day, and she often walked to the village church to visit his grave and speak to him of all that had happened since her departure. She missed him deeply, but she felt his presence in the world around her, and she knew it would have brought him joy to know that the farm was brought back to life.

Ada and Thomas spent the rest of their days on the farm with their animals and their children, and Ada never forgot the lessons she learnt from her father, as she passed them down to her own children.

OUR GIFT TO YOU

AS A WAY TO SAY THANK YOU WE WOULD LOVE TO SEND YOU THIS BEAUTIFUL STORY FREE OF CHARGE.

Click here for your FREE COPY of

'The Orphan's Opening Act'

CornerstoneTales.com/sign-up

'Set after '*The Orphan Star of the Dockyard*', find out what happened to Isabella, her two sisters Tabitha and Abigail, and the love of her life Daniel as they deal with opening night in America.'

At Cornerstone Tales we publish books you can trust. Great tales without sex or swearing, but with all of the mystery and romance you expect from a great story.

Be the first to know when we release new books, take part in our fun competitions, and get surprise free books in your inbox by signing up to our free VIP Reader list.

As a thank you you'll receive a copy of 'The Orphan's Opening Act'

straight away, alongside other gifts.

Click here to sign up for our mailing list, and receive your FREE stories.

CornerstoneTales.com/sign-up

LOVE VICTORIAN ROMANCE?

If you enjoyed this story, sign up to our mailing list to be the first to hear about our new releases and any sales and deals we have.

We also want to offer you a Victorian Romance novella - 'The Little Orphan Waif's Crusade' - absolutely free!

Click here to sign up for our mailing list, and receive your FREE stories.

CornerstoneTales.com/sign-up

Printed in Great Britain
by Amazon

42152750R00126